New Zealand Children's Literature

紐西蘭兒童文學
的書與人

Joan Rosier-Jones 著

石莉安 譯

簡序

　　原作者 Joan Rosier-Jones 是紐西蘭作家協會（NZSA）1999 年的總會長，我倆是合作寫書的朋友，這一系列的文章是 Joan Rosier-Jones（羅瓊安）應邀為國語日報所寫的，而我則在翻譯的過程中，試圖以一種再創作的方式來表現譯寫的文字；並且囿於篇幅，譯文較之原文也有部份節略。

　　本書中的 24 篇文章，都曾經以〈紐西蘭兒童文學的書與人〉的專欄名稱，從 2001 年底起在國語日報刊載過，於 2005 年告一段落。

　　如今這樣一本中英文對應形式的書，終於在我們的期待下，更全面地以雙語呈現在讀者的眼前。

　　這部可窺見紐西蘭兒童文學堂奧的作品，由於介紹獎項的後記篇當初在 2005 年完稿，為維持原文的樣貌，也就不再重新改寫，僅將 2005 至 2009 年紐西蘭兒童文學郵政書獎的得獎名單列出為附錄三，供讀者參考。其實根據文中所附的網站，這份每年都會更新的得獎資料，也就隨時在讀者的掌握中了。

　　最後，非常感謝國語日報社的兒童文學版——為華紐兒童文學的交流，搭建了這座橋樑；以及「秀威」給予這個出版的機會。

譯者石莉安　代序

前言

紐西蘭兒童文學的出發

　　在紐西蘭，為兒童寫作的風氣是相當蓬勃發展的。不過，這樣的風氣倒也談不上其來有自，也可以說這種現象的淵源並不久長，因為紐西蘭是一個年輕的新興國家。大約在西元 1840 年代，才有歐洲人成群地遷移到這塊「南太平洋中的新地」來定居。在那之前，原住民毛利人已經生活在這塊土地上有六百多年或更久。口語文學是毛利人的文學傳統，縱然他們沒有文字記載的故事，然而屬於這塊土地，這個族群的神話與傳說，就靠著口耳相傳的形式，代代之間一脈相承了下來。

　　那些早期的歐洲移民最初到達的時候，他們要集中心力在這片新的土地上討生活，根本沒有時間來顧及寫作。對這些前來拓荒的先驅者而言，大自然是冷酷無情的，因為他們的生存環境相當惡劣；套句中國的成語「篳路藍縷，以啟山林」，正是他們的寫照。拓荒者必須從蠻荒的林地，披荊斬棘地闢出一片可耕種的土地，他們種上賴以為生的莊稼，赤手空拳地建造自己的房子。等到生活安定了，寫作的念頭終於在人們的心中蠢蠢欲動。一開始大部分的作者寫的都是詩，要不就是寫些給大人看的東西，文章的風格大多模仿英國的傳統，那個他們不能忘情的祖國。倒也不能說就完全沒有人為兒童寫作，只是那些作品並沒有廣泛流傳，鮮少有人知道。

　　開墾拓荒的時期過了以後，大量早期的兒童文學作品，都可以在學校的期刊裡看得到。這些期刊是一系列的雜誌，針對六歲到十二、三歲不同閱讀層次的讀者而寫的。許多兒童文學作家，就是從為這些期刊寫故事，展開了他們的寫作生涯。

　　最受到孩子們喜愛的兒童小說當中，有一本叫做《落荒而逃的拓荒者》（The Runaway Settlers），作者是愛兒西·洛可（Elsie Locke 1912-2001），作品一直到 1965 年才出版。這本書問世後，就不斷地再版印刷，持續至今，任何其他的紐西蘭兒童文學著作都難以望其項背。這部小說是根據真人實事改編，故事是說一位住在澳洲雪梨的女子，為了逃避那個時常對她暴力相向的丈夫，不惜帶著孩子遠離家鄉，漂洋過海地來到紐西蘭，作一名拓荒者。她的冒險歷程驚險刺激，其中包括她如何驅趕著一大群牛，翻山越嶺地橫過紐西蘭南島的南阿爾帕斯山。

　　到了二十世紀的後期，兒童文學的著作不僅產量豐富，大受歡迎，而且獲得出版文化界的迴響，好幾個年度書獎應運而生，為兒童選出當年不同類別的最佳童書。2001 年的總冠軍是肯恩·凱特倫（Ken Catran），凱特倫先生的文筆十分老練，曾經為電視電影寫過不少劇本。他的少年小說《與傑森同遊大海》（Voyage with Jason）是根據一個古老的希臘神話「傑森奪取金羊皮」為藍本，所寫的那個南船座的故事。南船座為冬季南方星空上的一艘大船，它代表的就是傑森王子為奪取金羊皮所乘坐的船——阿爾高號。這個現代版的希臘神話用的可都是最摩登的語言，引人入勝的文字邀請兒童、少年或所有童心未泯的讀者，同來搭乘這艘船，與傑森和阿爾高號的水手們一起乘風破浪，經歷這趟高潮迭起的航海之旅。

目前這幾個兒童文學獎項的贊助單位是紐西蘭郵政總局。紐西蘭有位世界知名的兒童文學家——瑪格麗特・梅喜（Margaret Mahy），一直都是這些大獎的常勝軍。瑪格麗特・梅喜寫作的範圍很廣，從兒童的圖畫書到青少年小說都涵蓋在內。

　　她寫的故事極富於想像力，其中有本讀者的最愛，書名叫做《草地上的獅子》（A Lion in the Meadow）。她的青少年小說探討的則是超自然現象，有她獨樹一幟的風格。拋開她故事中奇情幻想的特質不說，瑪格麗特・梅喜本人倒認為，其實她絕大部份稀奇古怪的念頭都來自於發生在她周遭的事情。「但是，當然，」她補充道，「等到故事寫完的時候，這些人事物都變得不一樣了。這些想法當初是有憑有據的沒錯，可是在我發明了許多附加事件之後，結果就不是原來的樣子了。」

　　林俐・達德（Lynley Dodd）身兼作家與插畫家，她出了一系列的圖文書《毛毛狗——麥克賴立》（Hairy Maclary），也同樣享有國際的名望。麥克賴立是一隻毛茸茸的狗，整天調皮搗蛋麻煩惹不完，這一系列故事說的就是它一連串的糗事。這隻名狗可是大獲童心，世界各地的孩子知道的都愛它。

　　再提到另一個世界都知道的兒童文學作者，威廉・泰勒（William Taylor）。他的成名作《綿羊艾格麗絲》（Agnes the Sheep）是寫給七到十歲的小讀者看的，贏得過許多獎，包括一個義大利頒的獎。艾格麗絲被描寫成一隻瘋顛顛、壞兮兮的咩咩羊，是一號危險人物。這本書給排進了「好好玩的小河馬」那一系列的「愛須屯教育叢書」當中。《綿羊艾格麗絲》確實是一本名副其實的好書，而且是一本充滿童趣的書。

　　作家裘依・柯莉（Joy Cowley），已經為自己在國際文壇上建立起名聲地位。她當初為兒童寫作是為了幫助自己的兒子。愛德

華，她的兒子，從小和她一樣，學習閱讀的能力十分遲緩。《靜靜的人》（The Silent One）由雪瑞・喬丹（Sherry Jordan）配合插畫，贏得了 1982 年兒童開卷好書的首獎。這本以韻文寫成的書，如詩如畫，拍成了一部精彩的電影，於 1985 年上映，內容描述一個生活在太平洋島上的男孩，又聾又啞，跟一隻白色的海龜交上了朋友。

裴依・柯莉為各年齡層的孩子寫書，還兼顧到青少年的市場。和她同類型的作家有：暢銷書作者——泰莎・杜德（Tessa Duder），給琳・郭登（Gaelyn Gordon），楷忒・淂・幗笛（Kate de Goldi）以及瑪歌莉特・畢姆思（Margaret Beames）。瑪歌莉特・畢姆思以《外來者》（Outlanders）一書角逐 2001 年的紐西蘭郵政兒童文學獎，進入了決選，該書是一本科幻小說，十分的戲劇化。泰莎・杜德則以《堤姬・湯普森的演出》（The Tiggie Thompson Show）獲得 2000 年的兒童文學獎，這部得獎作品是關於一個女孩，如何一心一意地想成為一個名演員的故事。

紐西蘭的孩子喜歡閱讀，而且喜歡跟書的作者見面。紐西蘭圖書推廣局有鑑於此，特別著手「送作家到學校」這項計劃。如此一來，可為學童們提供了大好的機會，不但讓他們看到了心目中喜愛的作家，還可以和作家面對面地說說話。

每年在紐西蘭最大的城市——奧克蘭，都會為兒童文學作家及插畫家舉辦一場「故事節的盛會」。這個故事節有個很重要的特色就是「家庭日」。在家庭日的慶典裡，作家和插畫家都來到現場，跟各個家庭有說有笑，一起享受嘉年華會般的歡樂氣氛。現場安排了許多活動讓小朋友參加，他們可以製作自己的書，學習書寫各種美工字體，或者乾脆親自充當作家和插畫家，又寫又畫地編寫出自己的故事或劇本。

　　起步雖緩，但為兒童寫作和插畫已經在紐西蘭蔚然成風，成為最受歡迎的文學體裁之一。在這個兒童文學的領域裡，有太多的新鮮事不斷發生，更有好多的作家參與其中，教我一時無法勝數。好在我們可以慢慢來說，在接下來的每篇文字裡，再讓我一一介紹這些帶給我們新奇與驚奇的作者吧！

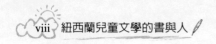

目　錄

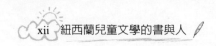

註：感謝國語日報兒童文學版編輯──鄭淑華小姐所提供的篇章標題。

瑪格麗特 • 梅喜（Margaret Mahy）

紐西蘭作家瑪格麗特・梅喜（Margaret Mahy），是一位世界知名的兒童文學家，她的書已經被譯為多種語言，都深受兒童的喜愛。她的第一本書《草地上的獅子》（A Lion in the Meadow）於 1969 年出版，直到今日仍不斷地再版。同時她一直創作不輟，許許多多有趣的故事在她的筆下，源源不絕地展現出來。瑪格麗特・梅喜原先在基督城的坎特伯里圖書館，擔任兒童圖書部的主任。1980 年起，她辭去了工作，成為一位全職的專業作家。

瑪格麗特・梅喜有一枝極富想像力的文筆，她寫作的範圍很廣，由詩寫到短篇故事，從為五歲以下的孩童寫的圖文書，到為青少年朋友寫的長篇小說，這位作家信手拈來，都能得心應手，受到不同年齡層讀者的歡迎，其中有好些個短篇故事，還製作成錄影帶，受歡迎的程度可見一斑。

幻想，或說是希奇古怪的想法，是瑪格麗特・梅喜作品中的要素。《櫻桃樹上的女巫》（The Witch in the Cherry Tree），《呼嘯下山的鱷魚》（Downhill Crocodile Whizz），《綠耳朵的女孩》（The Girl with the Green Ear），《象奶》（Elephant Milk）《海怪的乳酪》（Hippopotamus Cheese），從這幾個典型的書名當中，是不是可以反映出，書中的內容必定有些異想天開的東西？她時常寫一些有關超自然的現象，我們從以下三部青少年小說的書名，就可以看得出端倪：

《神出鬼沒》（Haunting），《危險地區》（Dangerous Spaces），和《分解鬼魂》（Dissolving Ghosts）。正如瑪格麗特‧梅喜自己說：「我要我的書名恰如其分地表達出，它是本什麼類型的小說，以及它是為何種閱讀品味的對象所寫的。當然也有例外，比方說我有一本書叫《逆轉》（Changeover），從書名就不容易看出它的類型，但是有個補救的辦法，我給了它一個副標題：這是一本超自然的幻想小說。這麼一來，就有了『警告』的效果，不愛看這類書的讀者就不會錯買了。」

故事內容雖然是虛構的，但同時它的情節發展，卻是深植在現實裡的。這種「梅喜式」的魔力，就是要把「真實」改頭換面成某種徹徹底底的「不真實」，卻還能讓這種如真似幻的「不真實」有說服力，教人信以為真。例如在《百姓家的巨龍》（The Dragon of an Ordinary Family）這本書中，一戶姓貝的尋常人家居然在一個偶然的機會裡，得到了一條小龍當寵物。剛開始養的時候，龍龍很小，後來當然越長越大，越大還越長，越長當然就越大，就這樣不停地長長長，一路大大大，大到不可收拾的地步，還在繼續地長長長，不斷地大大大大……終於市長忍無可忍了，先請求再命令，他堅持要貝家人一定得把這條大的不像話的巨龍驅逐出境。但是要趕走寵物談何容易，何況它還是一條巨大無比的龍。

接下來要介紹的是一本圖文並茂的幼兒書，然而這本書倒是十分「實在」，有一個平平實實的名字《一個夏日周末的早晨》（One Summery Saturday Morning）。故事的場景設在梅喜居住的基督城，她最愛的風景勝地「總督港灣」（Governors Bay）。這個故事的情節簡單，是在描述一隻母鵝，說這隻鵝媽媽，如何呼朋引伴地去追逐一群狗的經過，故事的特色在它的文字技巧，從頭到

尾，以重複的詞、押韻的音，表現出語言的節奏與音感。我們試著來看一小段：

> 鵝媽媽，團團轉，拍拍翅，嘶嘶叫，
> 拍拍翅又嘶嘶叫，嘶嘶叫又拍拍翅，
> 狗狗們，想不到，亂了陣也慌了腳，
> 在這個，夏天的，星期六的，早上！

「幽默」在瑪格麗特‧梅喜的作品中，扮演著重要的角色。有一首她的詩〈椅背底下〉（down the back of the chair），是在說一個爸爸把一串車鑰匙弄丟了，於是全家孩子出動，一起幫爸爸找鑰匙。結果他們找到了什麼呢？當然，一包大頭針、一把梳子，這些都還是想得到的東西，最不可思議的居然是一個又一個活生生的……待我們屈指算來：一個自稱是雙胞胎之一的討厭鬼，一個滑稽的小丑……，一個身懷藏寶圖的海盜……，還有……還有一條龍，不過這是條瞌睡龍，牠正打算好好的睡個午覺。而且不光是這些，找出來的東西還沒完呢！

作家梅喜熟悉寫詩的技巧，而且應用起來十分巧妙，她寫得開心，讀者們也看得高興。在〈椅子背後〉這首詩的最後一節，她運用「押頭韻」的手法，把每句的第一個字都跟「椅子」的「椅」合上了「一」的韻（註）。好，我們來唸唸看：

> 椅子，椅子，一心挑戰的椅子……
> 迷人的椅子，一群孩子的椅子，
> 擠擠碰碰的老椅子，

> 雞零狗碎的破椅子，
>
> 一時之選的好椅子……

　　換作其他文字功力不到家的作者，重複這麼多個「一」的韻，可能會很不討好，但出自瑪格麗特‧梅喜之手則不然，她照樣能寫得讓讀者看得興味盎然。這些反覆詞和節奏語將我們帶進了一個充滿童趣的世界，我們可以想見，這幫孩子全瞪著一雙雙好奇的眼睛，滿懷熱情地看著一樣樣活寶從椅子背後冒出來。你簡直可以看見孩子們手舞足蹈的樣子，他們反來覆去的歡聲歌唱，不斷地讚美他們那張出類拔萃的椅子。

　　瑪格麗特‧梅喜也很喜歡玩文字遊戲。要是找不到適合她用的字，她就乾脆自己造一個。《親戚家族四部曲》（Cousins Quartet）這套書，一系列四本，裡頭有隻狗叫「拉不拉貴賓」，這名就是「拉布拉多犬」和「貴賓犬」兩字的交錯字。書中有個神秘人物喜歡對著電話另一端的人唸咒語，唸一串嘰哩咕嚕的音，像這樣「歐萬尬本部踏破塔」。又如她有一本書，命名為《臥「海」藏「盜」》（Great Piratical Rumbustification），豈不就脫胎於成語「臥虎藏龍」，並且暗示這本書的內容是：有關海盜尋寶的冒險故事。在《十七個國王與四十二隻大象》（17 Kings and 42 Elephants）這本書當中，你大可找到她把單字變成語詞的例子，如「河馬媽媽」、「眾家狒狒」、「猩猩族人」等。

　　梅喜愛好文字的聲音，這點是顯而易見的。因而，她寫的故事都應該大聲地唸出來。每逢有什麼事情引發了她寫作的靈感，她都喜歡先講給周圍的人聽，再決定這樣的事件可不可以轉化為她要寫的故事。「我要先感受一下這件事聽起來到底怎麼樣」她解釋說。

　　比起其他地區的「梅喜迷」，紐西蘭的孩子要幸運的多，因為他們時常有機會見到瑪格麗特・梅喜本人，而出現在眾人面前的瑪格麗特・梅喜，可是很有造型的。她穿一身趣味十足的服裝，戴一頂蓬蓬鬆鬆的綠色假髮，看起來還真教人眼熟，就像……就像她書中的某個角色，難怪現場的歡笑聲不絕於耳。她最近在新書《冰凍幽靈的迷航》（The Riddle of the Frozen Phantom）發表會上，就為了配合故事背景的南極，特別以企鵝裝上場，有圖片為證。

　　瑪格麗特・梅喜的作品，在國內外都得過許多大獎，1993年，紐西蘭政府為表彰瑪格麗特・梅喜在文學方面的貢獻，特別頒贈「紐西蘭一等勳章」給她。瑪格麗特・梅喜有兩個成年的女兒，她目前住在基督城的「半島堤岸」，她的房子有個大花園，家裡有上千冊的藏書，還有幾隻貓，和她一起分享花香與書香。

　　要取得瑪格麗特・梅喜更多的資訊，可上網查詢，網址是：http://library.christchurch.org.nz/Childrens/MargaretMahy

註：原英文 chair，押的頭韻是 ch 的音；譯為中文「椅子」，則以押「一」的頭韻來對應。

裘依・柯莉（Joy Cowley）

　　當一群六歲左右的孩子蜂擁而入的時候，我正在圖書館裡面。他們隨即就被告知要在地板上坐好，乖乖坐好才能聽故事。手上拿著一本書的圖書館員，笑盈盈地看小朋友各就各位，說：「今天我們要講的故事，是裘依・柯莉（Joy Cowley）寫的。」一聽到這個名字，孩子群中揚起了一片歡呼，還有人大聲叫著：「裘依・柯莉！我們愛裘依・柯莉。」歡聲之後，「范船長的故事」從圖書館員的口中一句句唸出來，一張張可愛的小臉，聽得又專注又陶醉。

　　范樂最（犯了罪）船長是一個壞脾氣的海盜。只要有什麼事不順心，他就惡狠狠地大聲咒罵，罵到所有的水手都用手把耳朵摀起來，小貓也受不了，連滾帶爬地跳上船桅，再也不肯下來。

　　　　他的妻子很擔心，勸范船長說：「小親親，你看看你，你那樣詛咒罵人多麼可怕，你幹嘛不改改呢？」
　　　　「辦不到」，范船長說得很乾脆，「對不起，我的小花花，我就是做不到。」

　　不過，我們范船長的「小花花」有了個主意。她要她的「小親親」把所有肚子裡的髒話、壞話都寫在紙上，然後全部放進藏

寶箱裡,這樣一來皆大歡喜……只除了水手們不高興,因為他們本來以尋寶為樂,現在翻箱倒櫃了半天,找到的除了紙還是紙。

當年裘依‧柯莉剛從學校畢業的時候,依循父母的意願,很盡責地做一名藥劑師,一直到結婚生子以後,才想到寫作。當初她為兒童寫作是為了自己的兒子愛德華,愛德華是一個學習遲緩的孩子。

如何用生動的故事讓小朋友愛上閱讀,裘依‧柯莉對此很有興趣,於是從兒子身上,她幼吾幼以及人之幼,一路寫下來就是二十年,許多幼兒的讀本都出自她的筆下,有不少她寫的素材在世界各英語國家,都成了學前或低年級學校的教本。

裘依‧柯莉書中的人物,個個精彩。他們都是真實的人,卻又比現實生活中的人要誇大許多。比方說「丹」吧,他是個馬戲團的空中飛人,整天吊在半空中搖來晃去,另外有一群小氣鬼,成天計較個沒完,還有一個從來也吃不飽的「餓大個兒」,再加上一個愛用水東洗西洗的施太太。說到這個「濕」太太,她有個外號叫「唏哩嘩啦」(Wishy-washy),倒不是因為她愛哭,而是有一天,裘依‧柯莉在浴缸泡熱水澡的時候,閒來沒事,兩手這麼一撥一划,只聽得水花濺出「唏哩」「嘩啦」的聲音,於是作家靈機一動,就把施太太叫作「唏哩嘩啦」了。

紐西蘭南島的頂端有個瑪爾勃羅峽灣,裘依‧柯莉就住在那兒,在一個前後都沒有鄰居的農場裡,這個「與世隔絕」的住家環境,提供了她好多寫作的點子。有一年在瑪爾勃羅峽灣發生旱災,激發了她的靈感寫下〈落雨歌〉(Singing Down the Rain)這篇故事。〈落雨歌〉說的是一個小鎮,遭逢了前所未有的大旱災,人民苦不堪言,都十分沮喪。這時只有奇蹟才能救他們,又聽說必須找到那個會唱歌求雨的神秘女人,才有希望,於是鎮上的孩子就出發了……。

　　裘依‧柯莉很愛旅行，而且邊旅行邊收集寫作的材料。她有本圖文書叫《老鼠新娘》（The Mouse Bride），由大衛‧柯立思瓊納（David Christiana）作的插畫，文則改寫自一個古老的亞洲民間故事。內容是說有個嬌小的老鼠小姐想要找一個世界上最強壯最高大的丈夫，她想這樣才可能生出一群又高又壯的寶寶。她問過太陽，問過雲、風，還問過一棟高高的木房子，問他們要不要娶她。總之，這個故事有一個快樂的結局。

　　有些裘依‧柯莉的書寫得非常成功，欲罷不能的結果，發展成了一系列。〈愛哼歌的蓮蓮〉（Agapanthus Hum）就是一個例子，這個故事的主角蓮蓮就是根據裘依‧柯莉自己的女兒朱蒂絲寫的，朱蒂絲從九個月大，就和眼鏡結下了不解之緣。「朱蒂絲是個精力旺盛，活力充沛，又很開朗的孩子」，作母親的柯莉這麼解釋。「我不記得她到底弄壞了多少副眼鏡，有跌碎的，壓壞的，打破的，丟掉的。另外有一副更離譜，是掉在馬桶裡沖走的。還有一副給除草機碾了過去。朱蒂絲是個樂天派，她說她盡力在照顧她的眼鏡，可是當你成天忙著哼哼唱唱、還翻觔斗，能作多少叫「盡力」，也只有天曉得了。她這樣開開心心的過日子，我看了幾年，終於決定用自己甜蜜蜜的女兒作藍本，創造出〈愛哼歌的蓮蓮〉。」

　　裘依‧柯莉是一位時常造訪學校的作家，她去面對面的鼓勵小朋友，要把自己想到的故事寫出來。在〈大風吹的日子〉（The Day of the Wind）裡，她寫道：教堂附小的小朋友很會編故事，他們創作出來的內容包羅萬象，有關於巨人的，恐龍的，一個女太空人的，一條長二十公尺的熱狗的，還有其他的許許多多。可惜窗子大肆敞開，於是大風跑進來，二話不說，就把所有的故事都搶走了。好在最後，故事還是讓孩子們抓回來了，不過

鎮上的人也都看過了。尤其在大賣場裡，大夥兒傳來傳去，簡直到了無人不知的地步，他們都笑著對小朋友說：「太棒了！今天真是個不得了的日子，有這麼好看的故事，你們一定要再寫哦！」

　　裘依‧柯莉的作品涵蓋的範圍很廣。此處我們只著眼在她圖文書的部份，其實她也寫兒童書、青少年小說和非小說類的文體。她得過許多獎，最近的一個是紐西蘭郵局所頒發的少年小說獎，得獎作品為〈女孩莎德拉〉（Shadrach Girl）。她對紐西蘭文學的貢獻受到各界的肯定，不止在文學界而已。1992 年，她獲頒英國皇家勛章，次年又接受「梅西大學」贈予的榮譽博士學位。裘依‧柯莉是紐西蘭兒童圖書基金會的贊助者，她的網址是：http://www.joycowley.com

威廉·泰勒（William Taylor）

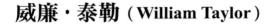

　　威廉·泰勒（William Taylor）的作品被文學評論家描述為「充滿田園色彩與小鎮風味的當代寫實主義」。我們知道，有好些紐西蘭兒童文學作家擅長寫超現實、富於想像力的作品，就這點而言，威廉·泰勒的文風則與他們大不相同。倒不是說他的寫作因此缺乏創意想像，其實不然，他所寫的故事都是情節緊湊、內容風趣、還洋溢著熱情。他有雙敏銳的耳朵，能夠準確地「聽出」角色間的對話，再者，強調人物性格的塑造，也都是他筆下搶眼的特色。

　　靠近紐西蘭的首都威靈頓，有一個叫樓而哈特（Lower Hutt）的地方，是威廉·泰勒的故鄉。他在那兒生長、工作，直到他決定「棄商從教」到外地去受師資訓練之前，他一直都是在銀行上班的。學成後的威廉·泰勒周遊紐西蘭各地任教，並且應聘前往英國倫敦，跨國教學歸來後，他選擇在饒沛湖山下的饒瑞姆地區定居，並且生活得豐富多彩，在此，他不但當上了小學校長，還從政，作了七年歐哈庫內市的市長。

　　為兒童寫書之前，威廉·泰勒創作過四本成人小說。提起這段往事，他總是很謙虛地說那些都是練筆之作，兒童文學才是他真正的志向所在。他表示兒童是最讓作者有回饋感的讀者，當接受訪問的時候，他說：「今天的大人是昨日的兒童，我想我筆下

能夠反映出的就是我們曾經有過的童心,以及在這個社會中成長的經驗;這樣的同理心,讓我有能力捕捉到孩童心中的希望與恐懼,歡樂與悲傷,並且能揣度他們所面臨的無法預知的未來。」就實際而言,長達二十幾年當「孩子王」的經驗,也讓威廉・泰勒稱得上是作好了充分的準備。至於其他生活中的體驗,當然也派得上用場,對此,他解釋道:「我有過自己的小時候,再加上多年來當單親爸爸養育孩子的『一手經驗』,我收集的素材已經夠寫好多本書了。」

雖然年近五十,才開始全時間的投入寫作,威廉・泰勒仍然是紐西蘭最多產的作家之一。他的作品名目眾多,不勝枚舉,所以這裡介紹的是八到十一歲的讀物範疇中,我最喜歡的幾本:

這類型中,最成功的一本就是《綿羊艾格麗絲》(Agnes the Sheep)。此書在 1991 年為作者贏得了紐西蘭兒童文學最高榮譽的一座「以色格藍」獎(Esther Glen Award),然後又在 1998 年於義大利再傳捷報,得到了著名的安徒生獎。如同威廉・泰勒多本其他的書一樣,這隻大出風頭的綿羊,也有許多不同語言的譯本。

艾格麗絲是一隻瘋瘋癲癲、壞兮兮的咩咩羊,也是個頭號的危險人物。她是老木匠太太留給兩個孩子的「遺孤」,是老太太臨終託孤,把寶貝羊交託給了裘依和白琳達,還再三叮嚀他們一定要善待艾格麗絲,就如同「親生的」一樣。所以,裘依和白琳達有多麼任重道遠,就可想而知了。艾格麗絲可愛也就罷了,偏偏她是人見人厭,討厭她渾身稀

巴髒，還一股撲鼻的臭味，這誰要不識相，擋了她姑娘的去處，那可好，她一頭撞上去，薰得你⋯⋯，到頭來你都不知道到底是誰臭。於是，寸步不離地看好她，就成了白琳達和裘依的隨身任務。不光是這些雞毛蒜皮的小事，這兩個保鏢還有個最終極的任務──其中有陰謀，有打鬥，還有謀殺，緊張刺激，好戲連連；原來老木匠太太有個又貪心又壞心眼的親戚，早就看艾格麗絲的那一身羊肉太「不」順眼了，恨不得一口把她吃下去。於是「羊命關天」，這兩個孩子要怎麼藏怎麼躲，才能保護艾格麗絲脫離虎口？哇，精彩精彩！在「愛須屯」圖書公司出版的那一系列書當中，你找不到別本比它更精彩的了。

《綿羊艾格麗絲》當中，涵蓋了人生的哲理，作者談到誠實與死亡，但並不板著臉說教，他用的是輕鬆的筆調，以若有似無的態度來傳達這樣嚴肅的訊息。

名為《急智針線王》（Knitwits）的另一本，也是兼具嚴肅與逗趣於一書，但是寫法卻大異其趣。一開始，就讓書中的主角查理·肯尼，以第一人稱的方式，大剌剌地道來：

> 今天早晨，我家的貓咪翹辮子了。
> 今天下午，我們的曲棍球隊把我開除了。
> 反正，事情有一有二就有三，果然，我媽說，
> 她就要給我添個弟弟或妹妹了。
> 總之，我有過不少「好事連連」的日子，今天不過是其中之一而已。

貫穿全書，和查裡分庭抗禮的就是這個作者埋下伏筆的小貝比，為了這個親愛的手足，作哥哥的不惜和鄰居愛莉思打賭，說

他可以給寶寶織一件毛衣。查理真懂得怎麼織毛衣嗎？大話被揭穿的他會不會慚愧的無地自容呢？要穿上那件七拼八湊毛衣的小娃娃，會不會也羞於見人呢？這可都說不定。

《急智針線王》談到「不要在乎別人怎麼想你」。本書的結尾留給讀者去想像，

到底查理跟這個家裡新添的成員要如何相處。不過這本書在讀者的期待下又出了續集，叫做《超級笨蛋》（Numbskulls），一開頭就繞著小寶寶打轉：

> 說到娃娃，大家都說，不過就是個整天吃啊睡的小東西罷了。我說這些人真是沒長眼睛，又忘了帶耳朵，要不就是少裝了個鼻子，不然怎麼會有人認為，小貝比好比初開的玫瑰花蕾，清清香香，含苞待放。咪！我來告訴你吧，我們家小貝比渾身散發出的那股味道，可真像那半爛的玫瑰花蕾，薰薰臭臭，含「鮑」待「發」。

查理實在有夠笨，笨到成天擔心自己做不來一個好哥哥。鄰居愛莉思看在眼裡，把查理騙到後院，說那兒有台神奇的學習機，可以幫助他成為拼字高手。查理二話不說就爬了上去，結果，真的出現了不少令人驚奇的效果呢。

用「文以載道」來形容威廉‧泰勒的寫作，或許有些「言重」了，不過在《超級笨蛋》裡輕描淡寫要傳遞的道理是——假如你真的集中精神在你要作的事上，你就一定做得到，但是，順其自然也很好，因為你得做你自己。在所有威廉‧泰勒的作品中，都有這個「寓教於樂」的意義，但更重要的是，內容都相當的詼諧有趣。

威廉・泰勒是紐西蘭作家協會的全國總會長（註）。他優秀的寫作才華獲得許多獎項的肯定。欲知詳情可上網查詢：http://www.bookcouncil.org.nz/writers/taylorwilliam.html

註：
　　大洋洲華文作家協會（OCWA）與紐西蘭作家協會（NZSA）在 2001 年 9 月締結為姐妹會，即由總會長 William Taylor（威廉・泰勒）與我方簽署協議書。之後於 2003 年 3 月在臺北舉行第五屆世界華文作協代表大會，威廉・泰勒受邀來台代表 NZSA 致詞。

泰莎・杜德（Tessa Duder）

　　泰莎・杜德（Tessa Duder）不是一個「獨善其身」的人。她時常跟有志於寫作的朋友分享她的心得，鼓勵他們要對這個世界保持好奇心，並且應該身體力行多做有趣的事，這樣才能活得興味盎然。「這麼一來」，她說，「你就有充分的素材可以下筆了。」這篇聽來有理的說辭，往往「說」易行難，但這位紐西蘭作家可是以身作則，將大道理實行得頭頭是道。泰莎杜德十八歲的時候，拿下大英國協 1958 年游泳比賽的銀牌。逐「異國情調」而居的泰莎杜德，住過倫敦、巴基斯坦和馬來西亞，她是一位經驗豐富的航海員，更是一個演技嫻熟的演員。所有這些經驗累積起來，造就了她成為一位作家。

　　泰莎杜德的第一本小說，《夜間航賽》（Night Race to Kawau），出版於 1982 年，內容說的是：一個參與遊艇比賽的家庭，就在起航後不久，作父親的被重物擊倒不省人事，然而這位一家之主是艇上唯一富於經驗的水手……。這個故事同時也為她稍後的另一本作品的特色埋下伏筆——彰顯出強而有力的女性角色，以及戲劇氣氛濃厚的情節。

　　泰莎杜德曾經說過：「作為一個兒童讀物的作者，責任重大，但其間並沒有什麼了不起的奧妙。相對於其他文體的寫作者，例如散文、小說，其中有不少是因著自己的欣賞閱讀，『讀』而優

則寫,由讀者搖身一變而成作者的。但兒童文學則因其主要的閱讀族群是兒童,所以這種從讀者中崛起而成為作者的例子,可說是並不多見。一位成功的兒童文學作家,必須先是善於經營文字的寫作者,而且懷著一顆不老的童心,可以在時光隧道中悠遊迴盪,又具有親和力,樂於和兒童多接觸。從這些特質當中,展現出的坦率真誠與不沾世故的正義感,就是一部優秀兒童文學作品的正字標記。」

泰莎杜德最成功的作品,應該首推那套「四部曲」的青少年小說,該小說名揚海外,故事的主軸繞著一名年輕的運動員艾莉克絲打轉。這一系列的獲獎好書,頻頻在國外發行,美國、英國、澳洲,都可見到艾莉克絲在文字中跳躍的身影,同樣地,本套書也被翻譯成多種語言,用不同的語音來敘述主角有趣的經歷。

就運動特長來說,艾莉克絲──一個游泳選手,正是作者自己的寫照。

艾莉克絲在第一集登場的時候,正在接受嚴格的訓練,準備參加大英國協游泳比賽。然而,在同一時間內只作一件事,對艾莉克絲來說是不過癮的,她依舊興致勃勃地企圖同時駕馭好幾樣:曲棍球隊少不了她,生活裡缺了她也會遜色。到底這種國手級的訓練,加在一個年輕人身上的負荷有多重?由泰莎杜德寫來才真叫「身歷其境」,沒有人比她更清楚了。艾莉克絲是個典型的模範,所有愛上這一系列書的青少年都拿她作榜樣。後來艾莉克絲的故事登上銀幕,泰莎杜德的筆發揮了「邊際效應」,洋洋灑灑地寫下有關電影製作的林林總總,引導讀者洞悉一部小說如何從文字到影像的過程。

戲劇和表演是泰莎杜德至今不渝的興趣,在她稍後的作品中都可以看出:內容的風格建立在這兩種藝術的架構上。〈堤姬湯

普森的演出〉（The Tiggie Thompson Show）就是一個衷心嚮往銀色生涯的女孩的故事。這個與自我意識交戰的女孩，透過學校戲劇社的演出，被電視界網羅……。本書封底寫道：「邀請你來加入『堤姬生平的頭一遭』一個最目不暇給的震撼年。」這段不凡的歷程，果真實至名歸，贏得了 2000 年紐西蘭最佳青少年小說獎。欲罷不能的堤姬還有續集，叫「迷惘的堤姬湯普森」（Tiggie Thompson All At Sea）。小說中的堤姬爭取到一個在宮廷劇中飾演女王的角色，可是當她越往歷史中探索，愈發現自己越陷越深，快要人格分裂了。雪上加霜的是，她又聽說自己有個同父異母的哥哥在澳洲，這其中的複雜錯亂，讓堤姬有如墜入五里雲霧中……。

為何鍾情於為兒童寫作？泰莎杜德回答如下：我將之視為一項殊榮。正因為年輕的心是那麼的寬容、能夠接收受新點子，易於取悅，我那些不盡完美的作品，才得以在他們面前「開誠佈公」。同樣地，如果我的故事沒有吸引力，或是不適合他們的年齡，他們也會毫不遲疑地讓我知道。

泰莎杜德喜歡「以文會友」，還從中發展出成果。我們上回介紹過的作家威廉泰勒，就成為她共同著書的夥伴。他們聯合創作過兩個角色：

這兩個故事中的主人翁，女孩在海上，男孩在山城，彼此藉著電子郵件逐漸熟悉，這樣的友情會演變成愛情嗎？且看這本叫作《熱線郵件》（Hot Mail）的書，情節是怎麼鋪陳的。

編輯也是泰莎杜德涉及的領域。她為青少年編了許多本文集，像是《墜入情網》、（Falling in Love）、《等待十七歲》（Nearly Seventeen），以及《紐澳作家精選集》（Personal Best）……這是一本從頭到尾都以運動員的成就為背景的短篇小說。

榮獲獎項和經費的贊助，對泰莎杜德而言都是相得益彰的事。這位在紐西蘭文壇很活躍的作家，也曾是紐西蘭作家協會（NZSA）1996 到 1998 年的全國總會長。她對於推動「紐西蘭兒童圖書基金會」的設立，不遺餘力。泰莎杜德 在兒童文學與圖書基金會方面的卓越貢獻，為她贏得了 1994 年的英國皇家勛章，以及一枚在 1996 年獲頒──以「瑪格麗特梅喜」為名的文學獎章。

泰莎杜德歡迎大家上網找她，網址是：http://www.bookcouncil.org.nz/writers/duder.html

林俐・達德（Lynley Dodd）

在享有國際間的文名之前，林俐・達德（Lynley Dodd）已經在兒童文學的園地，默默耕耘，又寫又畫好多年了。她曾是 1978 年兒童文學專案研究經費的得主，又在 1981 年以《英格蘭的女孩——杜魯希菈》（Clarice England's Druscilla）一書中動人的插畫，摘下紐西蘭全國金書獎的桂冠。但是相較於她後續開出的漂亮成績單，這兩項成就只算是起步而已。

1983 年的時候，一隻耀眼的狗明星誕生了。在林俐・達德的新書《當勞生的日記》（Donaldson's Dairy）裡，毛毛狗麥克賴立初試「狗」啼，披掛著一身茸茸的長毛，登「書」亮相。寫他的畫他的都是林俐・達德，作家塑造出這個整天調皮搗蛋，麻煩惹不完的靈魂人物，再搭配栩栩如生的插圖，讓這隻狗從紙上呼之欲出。作者有著一雙特別靈通的「狗眼」——也就是會觀察狗的行為反應進而推敲其心理生態的好眼力，再配上作者特別敏銳的好聽力——對押韻節奏有獨到的感受，如此眼耳並用的結果，讓這本書的語言「說的比唱的好聽」，連插畫都閃動著機智的電光石火。好書是不會寂寞的，麥克賴立的風采很快地傳揚開來，就在次年的「全國兒童圖書獎」大會上，這隻神采飛揚的毛毛狗獲得了評審委員一致的青睞，因而保送林俐・達德榮登后座，而且這個寶座在麥克賴立的護衛下，還一連好幾任。屈指算來，林俐・

達德總共寫過二十幾本圖文書，拿過不下二十次的兒童文學獎，尤其她的毛毛狗麥克賴立，在紐西蘭孩子的心目中，幾乎無人不知、無人不曉，知曉到了如數家珍的地步，舉凡與麥克賴立有關的一切，例如他的朋友他的仇敵，小朋友都知道得一清二楚。麥克賴立不但在國內大出風頭，還名揚海外，這一系列的書在許多英語國家都有發行。

說來說去，其實林俐・達德的書是很難用說的。因為她的畫就能說話，而且還「說」得詼諧幽默，其中「可意會不可言傳」的奧妙，我的禿筆不足以形容，在此就我個人最喜愛的一本——《麥克賴立的演藝事業》（Hairy Maclary's Show Business），來談談林俐・達德作品的魅力。

話說有一天，麥克賴立套著繩索被綁在樹下，這棵樹位於一個俱樂部的門外，俱樂部裡「貓」氣旺盛，熱鬧滾滾，原來一年一度的貓兒才藝大賽正在進行……。被栓在門外的麥克賴立心有不甘，他非常不安分地在那兒扭動著身軀，企圖掙脫綁住他的繩子……，雖然他掙扎成功，脫離了綁住他的樹，可是脖子上打的結終究沒法解開，於是拖著條長長的繩子，麥克賴立急急忙忙地快跑為上策。你可以想像，麥克賴立那副不管三七二十一的樣子，著實把那群等待上場的大小貓嚇得花容失色，於是眾家貓主人都同心協力地要逮住這隻闖禍的毛毛狗，但是麥克賴立滑溜極了，豈是輕易可以捉得住？他領著眾人團團轉，最後總算在李小姐面前「束手就擒」，不過，李小姐

可沒認出來自己抓住的是大家都在追逐的「寶貝」，所以接下來你猜猜看，誰獲得了這場貓才藝大賽的「最佳不修邊幅獎」？

　　然而，毛毛狗麥克賴立在《當勞生的日記》當中，並不是唯一的動物，林俐・達德筆下的動物園裡，包括一隻肚皮快貼到地上的短腿臘腸狗，一隻神態優雅，芳名「麥琳奇」的貓，還有一隻叫做「希得」的鸚鵡，是個大嘴巴，等等。另外有個反派角色，大名「爪留痕」，人見人怕，是鎮上最難纏的一隻公貓。這些個動物有時在以它們個別為主的故事裡，各領風騷；有時則一起上場，在偏重集體表現的內容裡，分工合作。麥克賴立有個外號叫「散散貓」，因為只要他一「驅散」起鄰居的貓來，立刻就能把貓兒們追得四處「逃散」。優雅貓「麥琳奇」就屬這些驚魂未甫的貓之一。只見高高的蘆葦叢中，「麥琳奇」閑閑地邁著優雅的腳步，忽然迎面來的……不就是麥克賴立嗎？但，別慌！他看起來也像是後有追兵的樣子，原來緊追不捨的是惡貓「爪留痕」，能夠讓麥克賴立也嚇得落荒而逃，可以想見「爪留痕」有多麼得意了。

　　林俐・達德從小住在一個極為偏遠的森林屯墾區。她的學校全校只有一間房舍，學生幾個而已。這樣的學校當然沒有圖書館，回想她的童年，林俐・達德說：「學校的資源太有限，我學習得靠自己找材料和發揮想像力。記憶中，我還不曾有過無聊的時候，我要不就是在戶外玩，讓心思乘著大自然的翅膀，要不就是在室內津津有味地『嚼』書，或者是廢寢忘食地畫畫。」好在當時紐西蘭國立圖書館的郵遞服務辦得不錯，讓住在「荒郊野外」的國民也借得到書。拿到書的滋味是甜美的，林俐・達德仍然記得：那種要去開信箱，期待揭曉的感覺，那種拿到書本的歡欣雀躍，至今想起依舊回味無窮。

　　成為一個專業的文藝工作者之前，林俐‧達德在威靈頓的「瑪格麗特皇后學院」教美術。如今她與丈夫和寵物貓「皮皮」住在郊外，這位作家兼插畫家表示，這個位於鄉下的房子，正好提供她書寫作畫所需的祥和寧靜，而且當她往家中工作室的大書桌前一坐，放眼窗外就是美麗的鄉村景致，立刻就啟動了她的靈感。2002 年，紐西蘭政府頒發「最傑出人士」的一等勛章給林俐‧達德，這可是一項最高的榮譽。

　　如要查詢林俐‧達德完整的作品書目，請至網站：http://www.bookcouncil.org.nz/writers/doddlynley.html

瑪歌莉特・畢姆思（Margaret Beames）

瑪歌莉特・畢姆思（Margaret Beames）從小就是一個喜愛閱讀的孩子，跟許多作家小時候一樣，時常看書看到「廢寢忘食」。「沒有什麼比看書更令我著迷的了，我常常越看越高興，就忍不住自己也想寫，我自己身邊也有許多事呀，寫出來是最自然也不過的了。雖然我越寫越順手，但認真考慮要把自己的文字出版，可是在我移民到紐西蘭來的時候，我當時都三十幾歲了。」

瑪歌莉特・畢姆思的故鄉是英國牛津，一個人文薈萃的地方；很多作家都當過老師，瑪歌莉特也不例外。從她的第一本書《綠石的夏天》（The Greenstone Summer）在 1977 年問世，她出版了 30 本書，類型涵蓋兒童圖文書到青少年小說。由畫家素・西曲考客（Sue Hitchcock）配上精美插畫的《花園裡的橄欖》（Oliver in the Garden）贏得了 2001 年的紐西蘭郵政兒童圖文書精選獎。她的另一本青少年小說《外來者》（Outlanders），則在同年同單位舉辦的青少年書類的角逐賽中，進入了決選。

根據瑪歌莉特的說法，她小時候的閱讀經驗，為她打開了通往世界的一扇窗，回憶起來，她說她可以從字裡行間跟來自不同文化、不同背景的書中人作朋友，他們豐富了她單純的小鎮生活。「就這樣」，她說：「閱讀豐富了我的想像力，開拓了我的視

野，幫助我了解這個世界。如今我自己寫書了，希望我寫的也同樣能給今日的小朋友帶來，我當年所擁有的收穫。」

的確，瑪歌莉特做到了。現在我們就來看看她分別在 1996 年和 2000 年為青少年寫的《拱門箭》（Archway Arrow）與《外來者》（Outlanders），兩本書也同樣是我的最愛。《外來者》是我買來送給侄子的生日禮物，他一拿上手，就關在房裡不出來了，結果是我們熱熱鬧鬧地在客廳為他「慶祝生日」，他則一頭鑽進外來者的世界裡拔不出來，連蛋糕都恨不得讓我們幫他吃掉就算了呢。

「豐富的想像力可以讓生活更圓滿。」這句話是瑪歌莉特親口對我說的。「不過更重要的是，我先把自己當成是個說故事的人，不帶壓力地讓想像力奔馳，說得順暢了再記成文字，等口中的故事化身為一本本書的時候，那份喜悅和滿足，就是生活中的圓滿。」

《外來者》就是這麼一個充滿想像力的故事，它不但引領你的思想天馬行空，尤其它還內容豐富，讀來十分有趣。這本書新奇、時髦，夠得上新潮，一開始說的就是一個「宇宙的大災難」，一個來頭不小的小行星掉到地球上，被它撞個滿懷的地球立刻冷得發抖，一下子，溫度陡然降落，下降的速度快的就像——一個鉛錘直直地往下落。於是，整個地球開始真正進入嚴冬，以前的北極如今比起來，實在是範圍太小而且冷度也差多了。現在全世界只剩下最後一批人還沒凍死，他們長途跋涉終於到達了一座半球形的建築物，這個建築物叫作「凍」，卻是唯一「不凍」的地方，是一個可以保護他們存活下去的人工打造的環境。下面的這段，就讓我們跟過去瞧瞧：

……臨進門的時候，她突然猶豫了一下，停住了腳步。「凍」就在眼前，她得好好地把這個「凍」打量一番。這個半球體的外觀是銀色的，構造這座建築物的材質，看起來像是鯊魚的皮。它昂然挺立，直聳雲霄……整個「凍」都沒有窗子。是該進去了，她依依不捨地回頭再望一眼……這外面的世界，還將眼光長長地投向那重重環繞的遠山。

「妳怎麼啦？」先進去的男人回頭問道，她短暫的遲疑停頓，似乎讓他有種錯覺，好像她隨時都會掉頭離去……

「噢，沒事，我只是在想，我們恐怕沒法再看到日出了，就算看到，也是虛擬的。」

……背後的門輕輕地扣上，無聲無息，要說有，也不過像「絲」的「絮」語一般，像絲絮般的輕柔。

　　這對夫妻是進入「凍」的最後兩個人。現在留在外面的，就是書名所說的「外來者」，據說他們長了一副荒誕不經的模樣，是人們口中的怪物，專用來嚇唬孩子的鬼怪。然後，物換星移，人們在這樣的人工環境裡，一待也兩百年了，這時候有個美術天才登場，她叫雷姐芮，是個學生，以下的故事就順著她發展。話說雷姐芮畫了一幅畫，畫得太「驚世駭俗」，無人敢逼視，於是雷姐芮只好把畫束之高閣，無法拿出來展示。畫雖然藏起來了，可是消息卻是紙包不住火，人們議論紛紛，謠言四起，都說雷姐芮一定是偷偷到過「外面」了，要不然怎麼會畫得出長相那麼希奇古怪的東西，於是謠傳雷姐芮一定會給住在「凍」裡的人帶來致命的傳染病……。

　　另一本要談的是「拱門箭」，讀者年齡層設在九到十二歲。書中主角史弟分和柯霖，正在為一個問題苦惱，他們想參加划木

筏比賽，獲勝的話可贏得一筆可觀的獎金，他們要拿來進拱門學校，學箭術。但是他們一來沒有錢，二來沒有時間，於是只好去找他們的死黨……不過，死黨中，傑米不會游泳，幫不上忙，安妮的媽媽連河都不讓她靠近……，崔西和司卡脫從來沒划過木筏……，但大家都把錢湊出來，報名費總算夠。如果一切順利的話，他們自求多福也就罷了，偏偏有個搗蛋的角色，叫「夏大語」，綽號叫大老鼠，他可是想了一肚子的壞主意，想要讓他倆退出比賽，然而他的第一個計謀就給司卡脫識破了：

> 「看！有人想弄壞這條繩子」，司卡脫指著被磨得起毛邊的繩索，大叫了起來。「還有這裡，看得出有刀子刮過。」「嘿，來看」，崔西也有新發現，「那條綁船的繩子已經被割斷了。」

　　瑪歌莉特‧畢姆思也是紐西蘭圖書推廣局「送作家到學校」計劃中的特別來賓，每次她到學校去介紹她的故事，都深深受到小朋友的喜愛。她不但寫的書很新潮，連出書的方式也很現代化，她最近的一部作品就是電子書，書名叫《裘瑟夫的熊熊》（Josef's Bear），網址上 www.ebooksonthe.net 可以找得到。這位有六個孫子的作家，如今跟她的老伴住在：紐西蘭北島的一個「雞犬相聞」的郊外。

　　如要查閱瑪歌莉特‧畢姆思的作品，可至網站：http://www.bookcouncil.org.nz/writers/beamesmargaret.html

雪麗兒‧喬丹（Sherryl Jordon）

　　雪麗兒‧喬丹（Sherryl Jordan）寫作生涯的故事，對有志當作家的人來說，是很能溫暖人心的。她在七年內，寫出了二十七本圖文書以及十二本小說，並自行完成插畫，可是真正出版的只有三本兒童書。至於她的小說，則無一獲得出版商的青睞。1991年是個轉捩點，她的第十三本小說《洛可》（Rocco）問世，這本在美國發行改名為《黑暗時光》（A Time of Darkness）的書，終於引起了讀者廣大的迴響。

　　然而書的廣受歡迎，並沒有讓雪麗兒‧喬丹的日子變得比較好過。自 1990 年起，雪麗兒‧喬丹就為所謂的「職業過勞症侯群」疾病所苦，各種不適的身體狀況，對一位藝術家來說，無疑是一種斲傷，說是災難也不為過。迫於情勢，她不但必須放棄她專業的繪畫，而且就連她當做消遣的種種嗜好，例如編織、駕遊艇、騎機車、絹網印刷等，也都不能保留。對於寫作，她硬是咬緊牙關撐了下來，她曾經試過在電腦上加裝語音輸入系統，但成效不佳。

　　儘管如此，她還是出了好幾本新書，並且為裘依‧柯莉的作品畫插圖。身為全職作家的雪麗兒‧喬丹，也時常到各學校演講或開座談會，甚至需要出國去參加研討兒童文學的國際會議。

　　國內國外，雪麗兒‧喬丹都贏得過許多獎項。在紐西蘭最大的一家連鎖書店——威特寇司（Whitcoulls），她有一本叫做《火之冬》（Winter of Fire）的書，長期盤踞在書架上，高居暢銷書前百名排行榜不下；此外，《火之冬》還榮膺為 1995 年美國青少年叢書之最佳讀物。到 2001 年，得獎經驗豐富的她，更是大有斬獲，她一口氣從紐西蘭、德國和美國的手中，接過七個獎。紐西蘭頒給她的獎，不只是肯定她寫作的成就，還包括了表揚她在兒童文學上意義不凡的貢獻，以及她在出版和語文教育方面所作出的努力。雪麗兒‧喬丹新出爐的得獎記錄，是維也納一個頗具聲望的單位頒發的，她的近作《超靜音》（The Raging Quiet）摘下了今年最佳青少年圖書的后冠。如上所述，她的書行銷遍及美國、英國，而且有好幾種歐語系的譯本在歐洲發行。

　　對於她的作品，雪麗兒‧喬丹有話要說：「所有我的青少年小說都是上天所賜的禮物。我並沒有刻意去構思它們，然而它們卻在不經意當中，鑽進我的腦海裡；佔有一席地之後，它們就開始『興風作浪』，許多的意境、景象、甚至屬於它們那個世界的聲音，都以『排山倒海』的姿態，向我襲來，我幾乎要被這樣的巨浪淹沒；它們千姿百態的性格教我著迷，我無法克制自己不去理會，於是我情不自禁地一定要將它們化成文字。」

　　這些讓雪麗兒‧喬丹禁不住要寫的故事，背景大多設在中古世紀，作者以可信度極高的文筆，清晰地描寫一些微小卻充滿感情的細節，來喚醒人們心目中對那古意盎然生活的嚮往。例如在《獅子的標記》（Sign of the Lion）中的一小段……「凱瑟琳取出一塊小方巾，把麵包和起司包裹起來。她把吃食和一小皮壺的水，一股腦都放進一個繩索束口的袋子裡，再將袋子綁在那位吟遊詩人的腰帶上。」

　　對以上的那段話，雪麗兒‧喬丹又補充道：「有些書在我寫的時候，靈感是突如其來的，某個角色忽然就那麼戲劇化地跳入我的視線，在我的心裡神氣活現了起來。」

　　筆者對她創造的鮮活角色，也印象深刻，我最愛的其中之一是旦吉兒，他是《周三男巫》（Wednesday Wizard）這一系列書中的主角，這套書是寫給十到十二歲的小朋友看的。話說……時光倒轉至 1291 年，當時的旦吉兒還在進行他的學徒生涯，住在一個中古世紀的巫術村莊裡。魏西老孃孃警告旦吉兒要提防三樣東西：一個叫「周三」的間諜、外頭的大城鎮，以及一條赫赫有名的龍。旦吉兒沒把老孃孃的話放在心上，他覺得這樣的警告只適用於他的師父范老巫師，於是他唸起了師父教他的咒語，要把警告傳遞過去。但不幸的是，這個咒語他可是唸錯了，而且錯的十分離譜，整個時空被他的咒語唸得翻轉挪移，他從十三世紀躍進到二十世紀，還降落在馬克家的後院。接下來的故事就發展出旦吉兒、珊曼莎和馬克，三個人友情交織的命運，旦吉兒極力要說服他們相信他是來自中古時代的男巫，他的當務之急是要找到回去的通路，他得趕快把警告傳給師父。本系列的第三本書，旦吉兒遇到了一隻會跳舞的熊──威皮。可是當他知道原來要讓熊跳舞，就是把它放置在熱盤子上，他不禁大驚失色。這下沒有別的事比解救這隻熊來得迫切，他急切地想要把威皮帶回珊曼莎的家。可想而知，這個救熊的行動不簡單，然後長途跋涉，把熊帶回家的過程更是艱辛。且讓我們看旦吉兒是如何一一解決的。

　　另一個我喜愛的角色是艾爾莎，她是《火之冬》書裡的女英雄。她的父親屬於一群被放逐的「亂黨」，現在只能做統制者的奴隸，幫他們挖礦開地。艾爾莎也是生來一身叛骨，又很有遠見。她十六歲的時候，就在心底發願，要讓自己這一族群的人過好日

子。於是她出發去找尋心中的桃花源，儘管路途艱險，還很有可能喪命，她仍然在所不惜。本書在封面上就宣稱艾爾莎是「黑暗世界中的亮光」。事實上，她也是作者在黑暗中所依靠的亮光。開始寫這本書的時候，雪麗兒・喬丹的病情嚴重，每次動筆只能勉強寫完一行。後來在書發表的時候，作者在扉頁向自己書中的人物艾爾莎致敬：「就是因為艾爾莎，讓我拒絕相信自己的寫作生涯已經走到了盡頭……她和我一樣都是戰士，我們一起向生活中的不可能挑戰……」

另一個不同類型的戰士，則出現在《獅子的標誌》（Sign of the Lion）這本書當中，時代背景依舊是中古世紀。就在主人翁明思特蕊誕生的夜晚，她已經成為父親誓言下的犧牲品，父親要拿她交換母親的生命。於是當明思特蕊十二歲的時候，一個神秘的女人來到村裡要將她帶走。幸好明思特蕊有個暗中保護她的守護天使愛默，儘管如此，要對抗冷酷無情的女巫革林瑟達依然不是件容易的事。

但明思特蕊註定是個「天將降大任」的人物，只是她必須受苦受難，如果她能逃出黑暗的森林，如果她能逃出革林瑟達邪惡的掌握……

雪麗兒・喬丹夫婦目前住在紐西蘭的陶瑞加（Tauranga），女兒長大離家了，家裡豢養一隻貓當寵物。如欲知更多關於雪麗兒・喬丹的訊息，請至網站：http://www.bookcouncil.org.nz/writers/jordansherryl.html

大衛・西爾（David Hill）

　　大衛・西爾（David Hill），是台灣許多人口中的「三年級」生（註）。1964 年他在首都威靈頓唸維多利亞大學的時候，獲得頒發「特優」級文學碩士的榮譽。他曾經當過十四年的中學老師，顯然這段經驗，對他廣泛了解青少年的興趣所在，頗有幫助。不過，他說，他開始寫作是為了要把自己孩子的童年留在文字裡。

　　大衛・西爾在 1978 年成為一位專業作家，但他同時也是一位新聞記者、文學評論家，除了專注於兒童文學的創作外，他還寫劇本。為他的青少年小說打頭陣的《賽門再見》（See Ya Simon）出版於 1992 年，從那以後這本書就頻頻傳來得獎的捷報。得獎記錄中包括 1994 年與今年兩度獲得英國的「特殊教育補助獎」，並且當選紐西蘭兒童文學基金會選拔出的，2002 年最受喜愛青少年書。

　　《賽門再見》說的是一個十四歲男孩的故事，故事的主人翁患了肌肉萎縮症，瀕臨垂死的邊緣。作者以相當中肯的心態來寫這本書，筆觸平實間不失幽默，卻又不過度的情緒化。

　　大衛・西爾接下來寫的三本小說，都在探究青少年的問題，那些在團體活動中不被重視的青少年，他們落寞的心態，和引發出的種種問題。每本書拿來作背景的興趣都不一樣，比方說《後踢》（Kick Back）就是一本與跆拳道社團有關的書；《安啦》（Take

It Easy）說的是一支健行遠征隊走錯方向的故事；以橄欖球賽得分的術語為書名的《達陣》（The Winning Touch），讀者更是一點就通。以上這三本書都發行於 1995 年。之後三年他又以一個籃球隊為主角，寫出的書叫《進籃》（Give It Hoops）。從每本書都看得出，作者對他用來當作寫作題材的運動有研究。下面我們就來看《進籃》中的一段描述：

> 人稱「得分之鑰」的馬克，又展現他強大的威力，在前場射出一個漂亮的空心球，得分！漢米序又吃了一個火鍋，搶到球的布魯克機靈地運球，傳球，得分！重回球場的馬理嵐，果然雄風再振，下一個得分的就是他。只見一連串的爭鬥、較量、攔截和圍堵，在兩邊的球場上激烈地進行著……

當然大衛‧西爾的小說並不全都和運動有關。「啟幕」（Curtain Up）的內容說的是一個參與舞台劇製作的團體。封面上甚至還有這樣的「宣言」從書中的一個胖胖的「四眼田雞」口中說出：

> 「我簡直受不了，幹嘛每個人都『哈』運動『哈』得要死，什麼鬼運動！我就不會運動。老實說，我又胖又是個大近視，我好沒用……」

這本書比較是寫給兒童看的，主人翁「阿本」終於發現自己有寫作的才華，是個不折不扣的編劇人才。故事是以日記的形式一篇篇記載的，還配上以線條取勝的漫畫，挺有趣的，其實該書就和作者的其他書一樣，總會不時地冒出幽默，請看以下的這句話：

「我把老媽做的胡蘿蔔蛋糕分給大家，美兒一個人拿了兩份。她還說：『我可是吃的很少，不過我少量多餐。』」

《衝擊》（Impact）裡的富雷瑟是天文俱樂部的一員。透過大型望遠鏡觀察夜空是他的最愛，但有天晚上，他看到的可比他預期的要豐富多了。一道流星劃過天空，然後「轟隆」一聲巨響，流星在附近墜落。於是，大家爭先恐後地要趕到現場揀隕石，一群人不只賽跑，還你搶我奪。

富雷瑟是一個很誠懇的人，故事開始的時候，他老實的被人喊作「傻瓜」。

「那個傻瓜從昨晚就呆在這裡了。」富雷瑟聽到別人這麼說他，他什麼話也沒回。可是五秒鐘以後，他就想到一個最適合的回話了，他應該說「很高興見到你，聽說你是每晚都呆在這裡的傻瓜。」他懊惱自己反應遲鈍，總是慢個五秒鐘。

小說發展到最後，富雷瑟成了英雄，而且有個金髮碧眼的漂亮女朋友。故事中除了主軸，還有個副情節，說到富雷瑟有個「中輟生」姐姐，跟男朋友出走，隨著樂團到處流浪；後來「倦鳥歸巢」，原來是懷孕了。不怕面對問題，是大衛・西爾作品的特色。現實中的問題大小都有，《衝擊》裡的未婚媽媽，《衝擊》裡阿本老爸的失業，還有《衝擊》（Time Out）裡的離家出走，凱特為了逃避父母離婚和母親酗酒帶給他的痛苦，成了個翹家男孩。

　　大衛・西爾對於寫作樂在其中。「寫作是一種感覺，你覺得你創造了什麼東西」他繼續說明，「是有很多人能做許多比你強的事，但是沒有人能寫的和你一樣，你所創作的就是那麼獨特，那種獨一無二的感覺很美妙。」

　　花甲之年的大衛・西爾創作不輟，去年就同時有三本書出版。最近的作品《終結後的世界》（Where All Things End）是一部科幻小說，預測的是 2040 年的未來。大衛・西爾住在紐西蘭北島的新普雷茅斯（New Plymouth），與妻子共度鄉居的歲月；健行、閱讀、為紐西蘭的黑衣橄欖球隊加油，都是他的嗜好。

　　他的書有法文、愛沙尼亞文的譯本，就連中國的山東也有一家出版社，發行了《賽門再見》的簡體字中文本。

　　歡迎登入大衛・西爾的網站：http://www.bookcouncil.org.nz/writers/hilldavid.html

註：
　　1940 年代，相當於民國的 30 年代，那段時期出生的人，即目前國人所謂的三年級生。

蓋文・畢夏普（Gavin Bishop）

　　紐西蘭南島的下方有個小鎮叫做「音符卡歌」（Invercargill），曾經以淘金著名，1946 年的時候，蓋文・畢夏普（Gavin Bishop）在此初試「嬰」啼。追溯起他的母系先人，是毛利人的後裔，這也就不難想見，日後在插畫領域享譽盛名的蓋文，自然會將好幾本書都定位在宣揚毛利文化。蓋文的繪畫才華沛然洋溢，坎特伯里大學藝術系畢業時，獲頒相當於碩士的榮譽學士學位。談起自己如何在創作的路途上受到啟蒙，曾經獻身美術教育三十年的畢蓋文，又將記憶拉回自己的童年……，他說：「我加入公立圖書館當會員，才發現自由借閱的制度，可以讓我享用這麼豐富的圖書資源，我簡直快樂的像進了寶山。『魔戒』當中的侏儒精靈哈比人，我九歲的時候就知道了，當我從一本期刊上發現了『魔戒』原著的摘錄，就對書中的奇幻世界愛不釋手，直到如今，我都還覺得這本書是靈感的來源。」

　　蓋文・畢夏普是個愛好旅遊的人，他的足跡踏過世界上好多國家，包括中國。1992 年的時候，他接受聯合國教育科學文化基金會的邀請，訪問上海和北京，發表了好多場關於兒童文學的演說，並且舉行工作坊。

　　比許多默默耕耘的紐西蘭作家幸運的是，蓋文・畢夏普成名得極為迅速，或許是能寫又能畫的緣故，他一「出道」，出版社

就爭相出版他的書，而且接二連三地把蓋文的圖文書帶到讀者的面前。蓋文的確是一個很會描繪故事的人，他用插畫來增添文字未傳達的細節，讓故事透過視覺的感受，更身歷其境地展現出來。

蓋文・畢夏普的得獎記錄不勝枚舉，在此提的是 1999 年「紐西蘭郵政兒童文學獎」，得獎作品為《傑克蓋的房子》（The House That Jack Built）。蓋文根據一首童謠寫出這個故事，其實有他嘲諷的寓意。傑克象徵著殖民地時期的紐西蘭歐裔白人，他們不重視原住民毛利人的傳統，以他們自行其是的方法在「人家的土地上」蓋房子，而且不單是個別的房子，還建造出一整個風格完全不同的小鎮。毛利人的大地之母冷眼旁觀，既失望又憤怒，於是……

其他還有好幾本書，探索的主題也是這位大地之母。毛利神話中的女神不少，得過紐西蘭 1993 年最佳圖畫書的另外一本，畫的就是一個毛利女人的故事，這個後來被奉為神明的年輕婦女，使用編織的技巧拯救她的族人，避開了火山爆發的災難。插畫的色調是陰暗的，呈現出一種不祥的預兆，直到後來日落的時候，女神才創造出色彩瑰麗的漫天晚霞，接著是次日的黎明時分，旭日亮麗的光輝正代表著新生活的開始。

當然不是所有蓋文的故事，都在訴說這個大自然間人力無法抗衡的力量，關於寫書素材的選擇，蓋文曾經表示：

> 「……不能不從市場經濟效益的角度來考量，在紐西蘭這麼一個小國家，書的市場必須往海外發展，所以要從全球的觀點來看……」

　　為了貫徹這個理想，蓋文開始研究不同的市場，眼光逗留在美國的蓋文，將領悟後的道理公開出來，他說美國需要一種「天真無邪又溫暖甜蜜的氣氛」。

　　為了營造這種氣氛，蓋文創造了好些可愛的角色，其中我最愛的是一隻小兔子，這隻兔子不但在故事中獨挑大樑，而且還登上了卡片海報，在紐西蘭大出風頭。「小兔子與海」（Little Rabbit and the Sea）告訴我們一個心情的故事，生動地描述那份期待夢想可以實現的渴望。小兔子多麼想要看到大海啊……每一個夜晚，他都夢到自己成為一個水手，漂洋過海……書中的第一幅圖畫就讓我們看到小兔子躺在床上，他的臂彎裡抱著一艘小帆船，床頭櫃上有一個模型燈塔，四周壁紙的圖案是各式各樣的船，大大小小的海鷗，還有高高低低的浪花。甚至連他的床罩都被畫成波浪起伏的樣子。這樣的畫境很容易就帶我們進入一個情景——小兔子滿心縈繞的就是大海。故事中的小兔子，鍥而不捨地問每一個他認識的人，大海是什麼樣子，最後小兔子的執著得到了回報，終於有一隻海鷗帶他去看海了……。

　　另一隻動物體型雖大，卻也一樣可愛，在《熊熊別睡覺》（Stay Awake Bear）裡頭領銜主演，故事裡還有一個配角也是熊。這部作品曾在 2001 年入圍最佳童畫書。我們都知道，熊是冬眠的，但是故事中的老熊熊和布朗熊熊卻想打破慣例，他們堅持「睡覺是浪費時間的」，所以當其他熊熊都準備要冬眠，老熊熊和布朗熊熊睜大眼睛不睡覺，並且計劃熬過了冬天，要怎麼去度假。

　　　「白天變長，雪融化了，他們開始打包準備出發。可是到
　　了火車站，他倆一齊哈欠連天……」

　　然後呢？然後這兩個熊熊在火車上，睡了一場好熟好熟的覺。他們……沿著海岸一路瞌睡，穿過山嶺一路大睡，越過平原一路打鼾……結果這麼一直睡下去，把個好好的假期都迷迷糊糊地睡掉了。然後周而復始，到了該冬眠的時候，他們又睡不著了。這是個很妙的故事，尤其適合講給那些不好好睡覺的孩子聽。

　　蓋文‧畢夏普目前住在基督城，女兒都成年了，他與妻子的家居生活正是甜蜜又溫馨；他的家在半山腰上，臨窗可以俯看基督城的全景，坐擁這樣一個寫書作畫的「王國」，真是「南面王不易」啊！蓋文邀請讀者上他的網站作客，網址是：http://www.gavinbishop.com

肯恩・凱特倫（Ken Catran）

　　肯恩・凱特倫（Ken Catran）在距今 28 年前為電視台寫劇本，就此展開了他的寫作生涯。一路寫來，他兩度榮獲最佳劇本獎，在他產量可觀的劇本中，有為數不少的是為兒童編寫的戲劇，駕輕就熟的結果，他毅然「轉型」，重新為兒童寫出一本本大受歡迎的青少年小說。

　　肯恩・凱特倫可說是一位多才多藝的作家，他的寫作題材包羅萬象、跨越時空，從紐西蘭的鄉間小鎮到天馬行空的科幻情境，從兩次世界大戰的歷史故事，到希臘遠古時代的神話傳說。

　　《與傑森同遊大海》（Voyage with Jason）就改寫自希臘神話中的「南船座」的故事。傑森王子與隨他乘坐「阿爾高號船」同去求取金羊毛的一行人，以摩登的語言再現古典的傳說，在凱特倫生花妙筆的烘托下，一部現代版的金羊毛奪取戰完成得極其精彩，還成功地為作者贏得了 2001 年青少年好書的冠軍頭銜——該獎由紐西蘭郵政局主辦。另一個改寫的神話叫做《金王子》（Golden

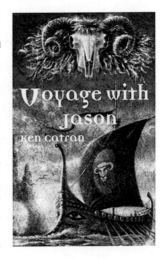

Prince），說的是「尤里西斯」的故事，在《木馬屠城記》的故事中，尤里西斯是率領軍隊圍攻特洛伊城的一位古希臘王。

《薯條》（Fries）一書的故事背景，十分靠近肯恩・凱特倫的家鄉。在這本標榜「當代小說」的書裡，提到一個生產「法式薯條」的食品工廠就快要倒閉了。

事實上，在凱特倫居住的小鎮上，真的有這麼一家類似的工廠。《薯條》是一本不折不扣的「倘若怎麼了……，你該怎麼辦？」的設問型小說。於是作者問：倘若薯條工廠倒了……，我們該怎麼辦？根據凱特倫的假設，薯條墓園的墓碑全會飛起來，所有的薯條幽靈會在鎮上神出鬼沒。但是事情可不如原先設想的那樣，還有個更大的陰謀在後面……在掀開薯條幽靈的神秘面紗的過程中，十四歲的保羅一層層地揭露了一個長久以來被人遺忘的罪行，並且還拯救了這個小鎮。

肯恩・凱特倫的筆下塑造出不少出色的人物。保羅就是其中一個。另一個叫麥可的，則出現在《與布魯密談》（Talking to Blue）一書當中，這本於 2000 年入圍紐西蘭最佳讀物的書還有續集，叫做《殺機重重的布魯》（Blue Murder）。

與麥可一起分享聚光燈的光彩的，是他的朋友——雪瑞兒，據描述，雪瑞兒是位「身材高挑、一頭棕髮，長得很好看」的女孩。《與布魯密談》一開始就以恐怖的氣氛吸引讀者的注意，第一句話就陰森森地告訴你「每逢星期一，就發生一樁謀殺案。」殺了一個又一個鎮上的人，布魯不斷地潛逃，在亡命天涯的途中，他不時地與麥可通電話，他是個「聞聲不見人」的邪魔。這部小說讀來令人悚慄，好在穿插了麥可和雪瑞兒的友誼，尤其他倆的對話非常有趣，展現了故事輕鬆的一面。

肯恩‧凱特倫所寫的科幻小說，《深水三部曲》（Deepwater Trilogy）和系列書《日光領域》（The Solar Colonies），都創下全世界銷售約五萬冊的記錄。

　　對於他的書被稱為科幻小說，肯恩‧凱特倫有話要說。「我發現『科幻小說』是一個誤用的名詞，」他解釋道，「因為實際上我寫的這類小說多半已成為『科學的事實』，我偏愛『未來小說』這個名稱，我喜愛作超前的觀測，把時光往前推移二十年，可是根據的還是目前的現實，這樣讀者不會有失真的感覺，卻又可以理解，依照現行科技發展的情形，二十年後可能預見的遠景，就會是我小說中所寫的狀況。」

　　《太空狼》（Space Wolf）就是一部凱特倫所謂的「未來小說」。這隻不知從何方星球緊急迫降在叢林裡的六腿怪物，引人好奇，大家都想知道，是否真的有這樣的動物成為地球的訪客。書中的兩個孩子「坦度」和「芒克」發現了這頭狼，「芒克」說明當時的情況：

> 「然後，我看到一個圓形隆起的輪廓，以及一排連結的長莖般的腿，其中有條腿在陽光下顯露了出來，腳下居然有個圓狀的金屬環釦。那個東西再次向我們紅光一閃，立刻就隨著它的腿退回陰影裡。這時一陣嘶嘶、啪啪的聲響傳來，聽起來是那麼的憤怒，充滿危險……」

　　許多本肯恩‧凱特倫的書，都以戰爭為探討的主題，作者將歷史的觀點用在現代場景的小說裡。《嬌點與亡命行旅》（Focus and the Death-Ride）可為其中的代表。這本書一開頭就給人一種「迷離幻境」的印象：

「外面是一片漆漆的黑，一隻貓頭鷹在四處尋找它的獵物。這隻貓頭鷹可不只是一隻夜行的飛鳥而已，它是一個妖怪，一隻口吐死亡訊息的怪物。」

這本書一方面是科幻小說，然而時空卻帶我們回到了過去。書中情節的構思巧妙，在男主角麥德跟布路斯和他的女友「嬌點」，談到他當年參戰的往事時，作者充分運用了歷史的想像。

肯恩‧凱特倫是 1996 年但尼丁教育學院的駐校作家。為銀幕寫劇本依然是他玩票性質的工作，如今他更是有心要把自己的小說改編成電影和電視劇。

紐西蘭南島坎特伯里平原的南方有個小鎮，這個叫作「外美特」（Waimate）的地方就是作家與妻子的家園。閑來無事的時候，肯恩‧凱特倫最喜歡散步、讀書……尤其是閱讀可以提供他大量啟發的素材，如有關恐龍、古代文明，還有外太空的等等書籍，則是他樂此不疲的事。

想多了解肯恩‧凱特倫，請上網站：http://www.bookcouncil.org.nz/writers/catranken.html

潘蜜拉・愛倫（Pamela Allen）

　　潘蜜拉・愛倫（Pamela Allen）是一位「兩棲」的作家，她不但能寫又能畫，而且很會得獎。二十二年當中，她出版了三十本圖文書。這些英文原版的書被譯成多國語言，如法語、瑞典語和日語等，行銷到世界各地。不同國家的孩子都喜歡她的書。

　　有一位澳洲的書評家梅格・所羅蓼（Meg Sorensen）曾經說過：「打開潘蜜拉・愛倫的圖畫書，我們不由自主地就會被映入眼簾的第一幅插畫吸引──它簡單的令人無法置信，然而卻可以讓全世界的讀者為之陶醉。」

　　這樣一本插圖簡單到虛實難分的書就叫做《幻想》（Fancy That）。說的是一隻紅色的小母雞孵雞寶寶的故事。潘蜜拉・愛倫解釋說：「這本書是給年幼的孩子看的。書裡面的文字表達了許多聲音，一個養雞場鬧哄哄的聲音，在幾里之外都聽得到。」

　　《幻想》裡的確充滿了用文字妝點的「音效」。母雞是這麼叫的：咕嘟、咕嘟、咕嘟。她的雞寶寶叫聲是：嘰噗、嘰噗、嘰噗，至於那雄糾糾氣昂昂的「考克……苦苦……考……」，則是發聲自大公雞。

　　「我是寫給那些還不怎麼會閱讀文字的小小孩看的。」潘蜜拉・愛倫補充道。「意思是說，我要看我書的人，大聲把字音唸出來。例如『噓』就是代表一種聲音，一個輕聲細語的聲音，又

如其他的：大吼大叫的聲音，笑的聲音，尖叫的聲音。還有喉嚨
裡發出來的『呼嚕嚕』，『嘶嘶嘶』或是『呱呱呱』。」

　　潘蜜拉‧愛倫的作品中時常以動物為特色。《我的貓咪妹喜》
（My Cat Maisie）就贏得 1991 年的紐西蘭最佳圖書獎。一隻街
頭流浪貓來到安德魯家，他想要貓咪留下來，於是就把自己會玩
的遊戲通通秀出來：

　　「我們來玩野印地安人，你來當馬，」安德魯跟貓說。
　　「不然，我們來假裝直昇機，像這樣，咻咻……颼颼
　　颼……」

　　這時書頁上的插圖顯示，那隻貓看起來很不快樂，對安德魯
要它東玩西玩的遊戲，都興趣缺缺。這隻很懂得自己要什麼的貓
趁機溜掉了。幸好不久，傷心的安德魯就找到了「解藥」，他家
隔壁的狗可對安德魯玩的遊戲樣樣有興趣。不過，這故事有個皆
大歡喜的結局，不愛玩遊戲的貓，卻愛回到安德魯的家，那天晚
上，它在安德魯的窗口「喵嗚、喵嗚」，安德魯毫不計較地讓它
進來，決定叫它「妹喜」，於是這隻貓就把安德魯的小床當成自
己的窩了。

　　潘蜜拉‧愛倫表示：「我的書希望讓讀者有參與感。讀過後
會產生問題，會有所期待，可以從中發現什麼，並且創造出自己
的東西。」她的第一本圖文書《阿基米德洗澎澎》（Mr Archimedes'
Bath），就提供一個很好的機會，讓閱讀這本書給孩子聽的大人
可以順便解釋「阿基米德原理」。阿基米德是西元前三世紀的希
臘物理學家，他發現排水量的原理。傳說中，他是在洗澡的時候
領悟出這個道理的。在潘蜜拉‧愛倫的書中，阿基米德的澡洗得

可真熱鬧，和他一起洗澎澎的有：袋鼠、山羊，還有一隻澳洲特產的袋熊也擠了進來。雖然並沒有放很多水，可是浴缸裡的水還是一直溢、溢、溢出來。

這本書雖是標榜「教育」，但實際上幻想的成份居多。「所謂寓教於樂，就是你能夠樂在其中。」潘蜜拉・愛倫這樣說明。「我總是把我的書當成是一段戲劇，讓讀者有看戲的視覺聯想，再推衍出更多的情節。」

除了「寓教於樂」，她的作品中也隱約透露出「文以載道」的訊息。「作為一個為幼童寫書的作者」，潘蜜拉說，「我用圖畫、用簡單的文字來揭露生活的意義。」《小黑狗》（Black Dog）出版於 1991 年，書中的小女孩想要養一隻藍色的鳥來當寵物，就對原先的小狗不理不採。這隻失寵的小黑狗為了要引起主人的注意，居然從樹上「飛」下來……

> 「她輕輕拍著小黑烏黑油亮的毛。聞到它一身狗狗的味道。感覺到它的心跳得很快。小心翼翼地，她溫柔地將狗狗抱在自己溫暖的懷裡。『小黑狗狗』，她低聲說給自己聽，『我愛你。』」

有時候潘蜜拉・愛倫用韻體文來說故事。那本得獎作品《馬客機先生遊大海》（Mr McGee Goes to Sea）一開頭就用英文的 tea，tree 以及 sky，by 來押韻，翻成中文意思如下：

> 馬客機先生喝茶，在一片蘋果樹下，他頭上有片天空，
> 一大朵烏雲飄過。

　　馬客機先生多勇敢啊！雨下得這麼大，他要去海上遨遊！他還好厲害！喝了半天茶，一滴都沒有濺到茶壺外面來。

　　馬客機先生的故事有一系列，遊大海是其中最引人入勝的，而且插畫都很迷人。潘蜜拉・愛倫擅於用畫筆捕捉她的情感、洞悉事物的內涵。

　　潘蜜拉・愛倫贏得過許多聲譽卓著的大獎，國內外都有。1983年的澳洲年度最佳圖書獎，她以另一本有關動物的書《誰把船弄沉了》（Who Sank the Boat）獲獎，次年再傳捷報，1984的得獎好書為《波提與熊熊》（Bertie and the Bear），成為第一位連續兩年榮獲該項殊榮的插畫家。

　　潘蜜拉・愛倫是紐西蘭人，但在她旅居多年的澳洲，頗有文名。我們再來看，澳洲書評人梅格・所羅蓁寫下的一段話：「她書中的角色都散發出生命，表現出活力的最高點，永遠在書頁上栩栩如生……那些擁有潘蜜拉・愛倫的圖書的人，都可能將之視作珍寶。因為這些書的確可以納入經典，成為兒童文學中的不朽之作。」

　　介紹潘蜜拉・愛倫的官方網頁為：http://www.bookcouncil.org.nz/writers/allenpamela.html 或者進入以下網址，http://english.unitechnology.ac.nz/nz/bookchat/current 這是一個可交流的網站，正在特別介紹潘蜜拉・愛倫的一本書「馬鈴薯人」（The Potato People）。

茅里斯‧吉（Maurice Gee）

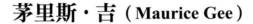

　　茅里斯‧吉（Maurice Gee）是紐西蘭很重要的作家之一，兒童文學只是他涉獵的一部分。現在我們鄭重地請茅里斯‧吉和他的兒童文學書出場……那一疊書有好多本，都是他寫給較年長的孩子們看的，是兒童小說也是少年讀物。

　　最上面的那本是他的第一本兒童小說，出版於 1979 年，書名叫《就在山底下》（This was Under the Mountain）。雖然這本書的內容純屬虛幻，但是場景倒是實實在在，就設在紐西蘭的第一大城《奧克蘭》。《奧克蘭》會成為這部奇幻小說的發生地，自有它「難自棄」的天生特質，主要是因為這座城就建在一連串的死火山上。有一群巨大的節足動物就蟄伏在死火山的底下，這群俗稱錢龍的軟體動物喜歡泥沼，所以計劃了一個驚天動地的大陰謀，它們要把整個世界都和成一大團稀泥，成為一個大泥巴遊樂場，至於這個顛覆的手段則是靠火山爆發，於是這些長得像蜈蚣的錢龍整日蠢蠢欲動，想要把火山激怒到怒氣沖天，這樣爆發一事就可以大功告成了。理查和伽歐是書中的兩位英雄，他們是唯一可以阻止這個毀滅行動的人物。因為他們擁有兩顆魔法石，可別小看了這兩顆不起眼的石頭，摩娑摩娑它們，就能夠影響眾錢龍的心意，任魔法石的主人擺布。

　　良善與邪惡的交戰，是茅里斯・吉的科幻小說中共同的主題。《半體人三部曲》（The trilogy The Halfmen of O）曾經在 1983 年贏得紐西蘭年度最佳童書。另外，這位擅長寫傳記式長篇小說的作者，為兒童接連寫出三本年代史的故事，分別是：零點的世界（The World of O），福地的祭司（The Priests of Ferris），以及地母的石頭（Motherstone）。

　　稱呼茅里斯・吉為前輩作家實不為過，出生於 1931 年的他，年逾七十仍不失赤子之心，童年總縈繞在他的腦海中，不時地他總回想起兒時的舊地，那個位於奧克蘭西方的韓德森區。幸好童年仍然可以在他的筆下重溫，讓時光倒流，我們從他的文字中看到一個在韓德森地區的小河灣玩耍的男孩。

　　有時他還會往下游去探險，去看看小溪的出口，那個叫做「外帖瑪塔」的港口（Waitemata Harbour）。他划的是自製的小船，木材則是父親供應的，他慶幸自己有個作木匠的爸爸。

　　不過是條普通的小溪，然而對茅里斯・吉卻有著特殊的意義。為此，他有所解釋：

> 　　那是一個奇異又詭異的地方，我在那兒第一次看到死亡。我從小溪狂奔回家，一頭衝進我家的廚房，覺得曾所未有的安全感，好一個安適的所在，溫暖而有情，然而小溪卻是另一個地方，一個險象環生，可以由你冒險，充滿刺激的地方……

　　童年的經驗為他的兒童小說帶來源源不絕的素材。《胖子》（The Fat Man）一書就以小溪的所在地為背景，在這本小說裡，身為胖子的主人翁長大後回到兒時的故鄉，但他不懷好意，想要

報復，要對當年嘲笑他是個小胖子的人展開報復。他一邊在溪裡洗澡，一邊在想如何找個幫手好做事。就在此時，來了個飢腸轆轆的窮小子，人喚「小柯林波特」，他因為爸爸失業家裡已經搜不出什麼吃的了，所以餓得頭昏眼花，看到巧克力就一把抓下，不料給逮個正著，胖子顧不得自己還在洗澡，先跳出來抓人為要。這下小幫手是現成的了，胖子逼這個餓昏頭的小子幫他去偷珠寶。然後事成之後……

> 「……這錢是給你的。」胖子的手伸進口袋，摸出了一個先令。
> 「我不要」，小柯林說，但是胖子不懷好意地笑了笑。
> 「拿著，小鬼。」他乾脆把那枚銅板往柯林的手心裡塞，還幫著把他的手指頭緊緊地扣起來。「咱們是有福同享，有難同當，老實講，你我現在是共犯，我們一起上那個老太太家搶劫，你還先進去幫我開窗子的，對不對？……所以……要是我被抓，你也逃不掉。咱倆一塊兒去坐牢。想想看，你媽會不會傷心啊？」
> 「會的……」小柯林嗚咽著說。

就這樣，小柯林逃不開胖子的魔掌。

事情越發展越糟糕，小柯林居然發現自己的爸爸也是胖子要尋仇的對象。這部交錯著報復和犯罪的兒童小說，剛上市的時候的確引起不少爭議，正因為作者的筆調太真實又太勇敢。但不論毀譽，「胖子」確實是一本讓人一讀難忘的書。

　　另一個別的兒童書也有的共同特點，就是故事發生的年代。顯而易見，那正是茅里斯・吉自己的童年時期，那個經濟大蕭條又逢第二次世界大戰的 1930 年代。

　　有些書則是根據作者自己寫的電視劇本再重新寫的。《縱火者》（The Fire-Raiser）就是其中的一例。這本書的情境設在 1915 年，比其他書中的年代都要來得早。話說小鎮上有個縱火犯，其實孩子們都知道誰是這個犯罪的人，但是要說服他們的雙親和警方相信卻是一件很難的事。本書中有個不尋常的角色「婆小姐」……「婆小姐」是一副骷髏……，不過在逮捕縱火者的時候，她是個關鍵人物。

　　如同茅里斯・吉大多數的故事一樣，《縱火者》裡也藏著教訓，讓讀者在不經意中去體會。背景在第一次世界大戰期間，故事碰觸到盲目的愛國主義和種族偏見兩個觀點。另一本檢視種族主義話題的書是《鬥士》（The Champion），時間則轉到第二次世界大戰。一個美國軍人來到鎮上，孩子們看他是英雄，是一個鬥士。可是在他們父母的眼中，他不過是個黑人罷了。這些大人極力維護自己偏頗的觀點，拒絕用孩子們純真無邪的眼光去看待他人，深怕他們的種族主義會在孩子們的眼中冰釋。這是第二部作者從他的電視劇所寫成的書。

　　2002 年，茅里斯・吉榮獲瑪格麗特・梅喜獎章，以及接受紐西蘭兒童文學基金會所頒贈的貢獻獎，這些獎都說明了茅里斯・吉，在紐西蘭的兒童文學和文字教育方面的貢獻卓著。

　　要知悉更多有關茅里斯・吉的書和人，請瀏覽下列網站：
http://www.bookcouncil.org.nz/writers/geem.html

朵洛曦・芭特樂（Dorothy Butler）

　　用「大器晚成」四個字來形容朵洛曦・芭特樂（Dorothy Butler），都好像有些意猶未盡，這位祖母級的作家，在坐五望六的「高齡」靈機一動，提起筆來為兒童們寫書。畢竟這年歲積累的功力不凡，她在文壇後來居上，很快就享有相當可觀的聲譽，不論是在紐西蘭或是在海外，她都以提倡兒童閱讀與培養文學風氣這兩項成就著稱，並且寫下好幾本有關這兩個主題的書，與作父母和師長的大人分享。《卡敘拉與她的書》（Cushla and her Books）內容是說一個有多重殘障的孩子，如何透過她所閱讀的書，生活得以調適並且得到身心發展的幫助。這本書被譯為日文，而且在日本贏得了獎項。去年，該書在台灣出版。

　　朵洛曦・芭特樂創立了一個讀書中心，針對有閱讀障礙的孩子們的需要，她還成立了一家書店，專門賣兒童文學的書。她曾經在一家出版社擔任童書部的編輯。當時她正決定要親自來寫故事，所以在童書部工作不啻是佔了地利之便。原本出版社都會為作家找一個插畫家來配合故事的發表，但是朵洛曦在這個領域的專業知識讓她胸有成竹，她對眾插畫家所知甚詳，所以輕易地就能為自己找到風格最適合的人選。

　　她是一位得獎常勝軍，國內外的大小獎得過不少。她認為作為一個作家好處多多，其中之一的優點就是：海外旅遊。「國外

一得獎我就有機會出國……要不在國內我也時常到各個學校訪問，去跟孩子們說說話，並且參觀過好多個圖書館。」

朵洛曦・芭特樂的作品彰顯出對孩子的親和力，她深刻了解他們的想法。與孩子關係密切是有淵源的，原來她是八個孩子的媽媽，還做了二十五個孫輩的祖母。

她的作品中，我最喜愛的首推《棕色熊熊巴尼》系列。起先，這一系列書是作單行本發行的，後來在 1998 年，合併出版了一大冊，就叫作《我的棕色熊巴尼》（My Brown Bear Barney）。

故事是這麼開場的，一個小女孩帶著她的玩具熊巴尼，不管上哪兒都帶著它。她要去跟朋友玩的時候，得帶上一大堆東西，有腳踏車，她的老狗狗，兩個蘋果，一雙雨鞋，還有她的棕色熊熊。總之，巴尼老是跟著她，逛街跟著她，睡覺也跟著她，跟她一塊兒去海灘，又一起上奶奶家。但是，有一天媽媽告訴小女孩，等她開始上學，巴尼就不能再跟了。小女孩聽了心思和眼睛一塊兒轉，她答應媽媽會跟巴尼一起考慮看看。

在最後的三個故事裡，巴尼真的跟去上學了，只不過它不能進教室，必須待在洗手間裡。這時班上正在準備一場同樂會，要表演給家長和朋友們看，而小女孩一心記掛著她的熊熊，想到它孤伶伶地留在她的書包裡，被吊在廁所的掛鉤上，她的心裡好難過。可她萬萬沒有想到，巴尼其實已經跑出去了，它自己去演出一場「小熊歷險記」。在這本書裡，圖片與文字之間全然相互矛盾，很巧妙地彼此唱著反調。

朵洛曦・芭特樂對玩具熊，顯然情有獨鍾，她讓一個又一個的熊熊登場，另一本用熊來當主題的書叫做《老熊－海克特》（Hector, An Old Bear）。這本書的插畫美侖美奐，全都出自琳・柯蕾格樂（Lyn Kriegler）的畫筆之下，表現出一個二十世紀初的

家庭，一個名叫「雅麗珊德菈」的小女兒，以及她心愛的老熊「海克特」。一場意外讓「海克特」傷痕累累，雖然大家都盡力要修復它，看來還是回天乏術了。於是雅麗珊德菈的父親為她買了一隻新的熊。但她是否就此拋棄海克特，讓新熊取代它的地位呢？不！她把新熊給了她的弟弟，然後：

　　她舉起她自己的老熊熊，
　　她自己的熊，她自己的熊。
　　當你有了自己的熊，
　　你就不會要其他的熊熊。

　　文中的句子，都是刻意重複的。為的要讓這本書充滿律動，好唸又能吸引小朋友的注意。書中的插圖都畫得十分細膩，描繪出那個走進歷史的時代──殖民地時期的廚房，廚房裡的廚子，廚子用來烘培的舊式鐵爐，還有那個式樣老舊的搖擺木馬。

　　《露露》（Lulu），是一本同樣由琳·柯蕾格樂配上插畫的書。露露是一隻在住家附近徘徊的流浪貓。當所有的家貓都被寵壞了，一個個都懶洋洋的沒什麼個性，相形之下，露露是既冷靜又勇敢。當其他的貓都在吃魚舔牛奶的時候，露露得辛辛苦苦地從垃圾箱裡找食物，好在那些等著她的食物都還挺新鮮的呢。

　　朵洛曦·芭特樂表示，她從小受到母親與祖母的啟迪，她說：「母親告訴我們很多她童年的故事，那些故事令人悠然神往。跟我們同住的奶奶也是一位說故事的好手，許多早期先人搭船從歐洲來紐西蘭的故事，都從她口中生動地描述出來。」

　　目前朵洛曦・芭特樂住在奧克蘭的西岸，一棟古色古香的房子裡。這棟老屋同時也是一座大型的兒童圖書室，她住在附近的眾多孫兒以及社區的孩童，都受惠於這份珍貴的禮物。

　　以下是作家的專訪網頁：http://christchurchcitylibraries.com/Kids/ChildrensAuthors/DorothyButler.asp

挪門・比爾波羅（Norman Bilbrough）

　　挪門・比爾波羅（Norman Bilbrough）的寫作生涯已長達三十年，同時他還在小說的領域中成為一位得獎的作家，贏得過兩次由紐西蘭的周日星報主辦的短篇小說大賽。千禧年的時候，他以一篇〈哈囉紐西蘭先生〉（Hello Mr New Zealand）在國際筆會的徵文比賽中脫穎而出，獲得紐西蘭的首獎，這篇作品可是作者的親身經歷，取材自 1980 年代在香港的越南難民營中的所見所聞。挪門見多識廣，又擅長利用生花妙筆，將他林林總總的見識寫成一篇篇受歡迎的兒童以及青少年的讀物。

　　挪門寫的故事大多都刊登在中小學期刊（School Journal）當中，這份刊物全國發行，讀者眾多。1998 年挪門以「難吃的寫實主義」（Yuk Realism）為題，出版了一本選集，名為《狗味道及其他》（Dog Breath and Other Stories）。在此一提，筆者在本系列介紹的作家中，有不少早期都當過老師，挪門也不例外，他最初投入的工作就是教書。喜愛為兒童寫作的挪門曾經表示：「兒童需要閱讀那些簡單的故事，但是得配合精彩的情節。孩童通常比成人讀者更容易呼應他們的想像力，因此，舉凡荒誕不經的故事，希奇古怪的想法，以及不可思議的人物，通通都可以呈現在文字裡交由兒童去想像。所以為兒童寫作的

時候，我任由思想天馬行空，無需拐彎抹角，我直截了當地就邀請小讀者進入我的想像空間。」他的故事，的確，充滿想像。

在他的小說中，出現過這麼一個例子。這本《鳥人獨自在打獵》（The Birdman Hunts Alone），曾經入圍 1994 年的「標干兒童讀物大獎」。這個故事的開頭平淡無奇，話說有三個表姐弟在奧克蘭北方的一個農場上度假，不過這個平凡的開始所佔的篇幅並不長，沒多久，變化向這個平靜的農莊撲來，這整個情景就有了改變。原本好端端在照片中的女人突然走出來，對臥室中準備就寢的托比施展催眠術。只怪托比換了個新環境，一時睡不著，他就瞪著那張掛在牆上的相片看，看著看著居然把影像中的女人給看活了，這個變得「生動」的女人開口說話了，字字句句在托比的腦海中流轉，到底是真是假，究竟是夢是幻？托比的意識矇矇朧朧，只想沉醉在一個虛幻的世界裡。後來，這個催眠女巫把表姐弟三個都帶進她的奇異世界——「袄地」，有首歌謠在這兒流傳已久，「鳥人獨自在打獵」這句話就出現在歌謠當中，這是個充滿傳奇的地方。

然後女巫奉命帶他們三人飛越千山萬水去尋找奇異世界的萬邦領袖——那個失蹤已久的「曼達克」，只有他才能幫助大家重返「佳樂地」，回到那個曾經歡樂又公正的國度。他們的旅程充滿驚險、危機處處，他們一一經歷許多奇怪的地方，連名字都很奇怪，譬如叫作「大風的牙齒」，「不說話的高塔」等等。他們好不容易從一個戰場上脫身，又見一個「過河卒子」迎面襲來，但是找來找去，就是找不到「曼達克」。在歷經重重冒險之後，他們從中認清自己的強勢與弱點，學到了珍貴的教訓。最後那首歌謠成真，他們與鳥人一同歸來，而鳥人就是「曼達克」。

「狗味道」中的故事，足以一絲不苟地喚起讀者青少年時期的記憶，全書洋溢著幽默。封面上的廣告詞是這麼說的：這裡有些故事該逆向思考，但所有的故事都所向無敵……在標題故事裡，主角麥特得到一份理想的工作——當「品味員」。結果麥特對品嚐的食物吃上了癮，吃成了一個大胖子。另外一個麻煩則是，麥特發現當地所有的狗都對他緊追不捨，全愛上他一身的「狗味道」。原來他負責嚐味的東西，居然是狗食品。難怪挪門・比爾波羅稱自己這一系列的故事為「難吃的寫實主義」。麥特的爸爸是一個很討喜的角色，分量僅次於主角，故事中是這麼介紹他的：

> 然後，只見那個老頭把嘴巴貼在玻璃上，留下了一個大大濕濕的口印子。
> 「不要那個樣子，爸爸。」我裝腔作勢地大聲喊著說。

同一本選集的另一個故事裡，馬可的爸爸在他兩歲的時候就離開了。長大後的馬可去看爸爸，發現他是個素食者，這讓喜愛吃牛排的馬可很為難，於是每次要看爸爸他都能拖就拖。可是媽媽卻堅持要他關掉熱門音樂去看爸爸，因為她需要清靜。然而，這次探訪爸爸，事情有了轉機。爸爸有了一個新女友，她很了解馬可，還帶他去騎馬。等馬可回家以後，甚至連媽媽也有了轉變。

挪門・比爾波羅的短篇故事，多數都在探討現代家庭各種問題，雖然有些主題很沉重，但挪門以輕鬆幽默的筆觸來處理這些嚴肅的問題。在另一篇名為〈鬼作家〉（The Ghost of Katherine Mansfield）的故事中，麥特是一個鬱鬱寡歡的孩子，因為他媽媽也離家出走了，跑去跟一個阿姨住在一起。麥特逃學去找媽媽，

在渡輪上遇到紐西蘭國寶級名作家凱瑟琳·曼思菲爾（Katherine Mansfield）的鬼魂。鬼作家找不到回老家的路，麥特幫忙領路，一路上曼思菲爾告訴麥可關於她生平的故事，由於她也有麥可媽媽類似的家庭問題，所以自然而然地幫助麥可解決了他心裡的困惑。

再一個與現代家庭有關的篇名叫〈莫斯里的老爹〉（Mosley's Dad），故事中，十歲的莫斯里第一次見到自己的爸爸。乍見之下，莫斯里真是大失所望，他原本期待看到一個年輕又長得很「酷」的爸爸，不料爸爸竟是一個不修邊幅的半百老頭。不過後來他發現爸爸也很喜歡打板球，於是一場球賽下來，父子感情大有進步，莫斯里再也不嫌爸爸了。

挪門·比爾波羅說，他的想法都是從感覺而來。「一種感覺，或是一個想法，就這樣突如其來地一把抓住了我。」比如說《火星人》（Mars Bar）就是一個偶然興起的科幻念頭，驅使他寫下的一本書。一個名叫火星的小孩來上學，和他作朋友的杰森發現他吃電當午餐，嚇了一大跳，放學後，又看到這個怪小孩搭乘飛碟回家。

首都威靈頓有一大片叢林保留區，挪門·比爾波羅就住在保留區的對面。每天早晨他都在鳥語啼囀中醒來，住在這樣一個接近大自然的環境中，他寫小說、作評述，為文學努力不輟。

查詢挪門比爾波羅，請上網站：http://www.bookcouncil.org.nz/writers/bilbroughn.html

芙蘿珥・畢蕾（Fleur Beale）

據說 J・K・羅琳（J・K・Rowling）一開始寫《哈利波特》的時候沒有用全名，因為擔心男孩子不愛看女作家寫的小說，而她這一系列的故事又特別對男孩子投其所好。類似這樣子的名字情結，倒是不會發生在芙蘿珥・畢蕾（Fleur Beale）身上，雖然她的名字明顯地相當女性化，因為芙蘿珥就是法文「花」的意思，但她的許多書都是以男孩子為對象，而這些讀者都對她的書愛不釋手。

我們就先來看看她的小說中有關青少年的話題——在《討「駕」還價》（Driving a Bargain）一書中，一群半大不小的男孩花了一整個暑假學開車，開一部要報廢的老爺車，他們把小牧場當練車場，整天在那兒開來開去。其中一個叫湯姆士的，發表他第一次開車的經驗：

> 「那個下午我第一次鑽進那部車。我一發動引擎就停不下來！我開著車子在牧場裡橫衝直撞，自己也大聲呼喊，放聲尖叫。這時眼前出現了一個轉角！我連忙把輪子轉向右邊，又打向左邊。我一踩油門，發出一個怪聲。我一定是哪裡做錯了，這才誤打誤撞地把車子停了下來。」

以上這本書在 1995 年進入紐西蘭全國最佳少年小說類的決選，探討的正是芙蘿珥・畢蕾一向關心的主題——青少年有認清自己歸屬感的需要。

1999 年出版的《勢在必贏》（Playing to Win）內容關於紐西蘭最愛的運動——橄欖球賽。小鎮上的丹尼初來乍到，他覺得自己受到排擠，但他希望站在塔德——那個本地男孩——的身邊的時候，看起來很炫，這樣他才可以贏得那個可愛的艾麗絲對他的注意。他積極地組成了一個橄欖球隊，但是事情不如想像中的容易，因為他有別人所沒有的重責大任。他必須幫媽媽照顧孩子——他的一對雙胞胎小妹妹。每天去學校接她們，然後看管這兩個妹妹就是他的例行工作。他很寵這兩個小跟班，不但隨身「攜帶」，而且還允許她們「撒野」，任由她們跳上跳下，容忍她們的搗蛋惡作劇。其實丹尼的可愛就在這個地方，這也是他的人格特質——十分的寬宏大量。一天下午，他要去練球，而兩個妹妹也非得帶去不可。

> 塔德楞了一下，他花了兩秒鐘的時間，才反應過來我帶著妹妹來練球，於是他開始揶揄我，現是咩咩咩的學羊叫，說我是隻母山羊，然後改口說我是奶爸，後來又乾脆叫我是「媽咪」。我默默聽著，什麼話也沒說。我想我不開口則已，一旦開始跟塔德回嘴，我的脾氣也會爆發，到頭來只有把事情弄到不可收拾的地步。……我身穿 8 號球衣，打側翼手的位置，我從側面攻擊達陣，並射門得分……就在兩隊並列爭球，我搶到球仆倒的時候，塔德趁機端了我一腳，他那隻釘鞋立刻就在我背上留下一個「漂亮的」圖案。

接下來又是個違規的把戲——他用手肘頂撞我的喉部企圖攔截。我將手舉起又彎下腰來咳嗽……

「哥哥！哥哥！你受傷了！」我的兩個妹妹瘋狂地衝過草地，向我撲過來。「就算他先前沒事，這回可真傷到了。」教練喃喃地說……

　　如同大部分我們以前所討論到的作家，芙蘿珥‧畢蕾也是當老師出身。她從二十年前就開始為廣播電臺撰寫兒童故事。芙蘿珥‧畢蕾表示，作為一個作家最過癮的就是「可以作自己的老闆。能夠打造一個屬於自己的世界，然後踏上冒險之旅，其中自己所創造的驚險刺激，可能在現實生活中你終其一生都不可能遇到的。」

　　芙蘿珥‧畢蕾當然不只是以男孩子為預設的讀者群，她有不少的書都是為女孩子而寫的。在《不知名的幸運》（Lucky for Some）裡，主人翁就是一個女孩，她心不甘情不願地要隨父母從城市搬到鄉村。城市有她所需要的一切：許多的朋友，變化多端的舞蹈課，還有時髦的髮型設計師，以及各種「垃圾食物」，這才是所謂的「生活」。反之，鄉村能提供她什麼？充其量不過是：一個可以當古蹟的「新」家，一群臭烘烘的牛，一片單調乏味的青草地，最多不過能踢踢橄欖球吧，這叫什麼生活？簡直沒有生活。但是幸好這個可怕的夢魘並沒有成真。經過一陣搖擺不定的初期，蕾西發現鄉村生活並非想像中的那麼糟糕。她甚至還跟一頭叫「舞蹈家」的母牛交上朋友——並且還學會了如何照顧一頭牛。她領著「舞蹈家」作繞場練習，準備要在農業節那天大顯身手，可是「舞蹈家」是一隻有個性的牛，也不輕易任人擺佈，不過，等日子到的時候奇蹟出現了，蕾西領著「舞蹈家」作了一場完美的演出。

「如果你夠幸運的話，」芙蘿珥‧畢蕾這麼說，「好點子就會出其不意地從天而降。」有時候許多想法你必須從內心深處去挖掘，又有時候它們自然從發生過的事情中跳脫出來，《不知名的幸運》就是如此成型的一本書。對於這個故事的緣起她解釋道：有一年我家房子改建，我們曾經在一個百年的鄉村老屋借住過，故事的背景大多依據那段生活經驗。當時我女兒分別是十歲、十二歲，為了參加農業節的慶典，她們養過小牛、山羊各一隻。就像我書中的蕾西不會領牛繞場一樣，她本來是很怕那頭小牛的，結果就在表演的那一天，為了某種不知名的原因，她居然表現得極其完美還贏得了那座「最佳領場人」的獎杯。

1999 年是芙蘿珥‧畢蕾豐收的一年。位於全國第五大城的但尼丁教育學院邀請她擔任駐校作家，同時她還接受紐西蘭郵政局主辦的年度兒童文學獎頒發的榮譽獎，肯定她在少年小說方面的成就。《我不是以斯帖》（I Am Not Esther），這本引用聖經舊約中一位廣為人知的女子「以斯帖」為名的書，就在講一個女孩如何在她寄居的基督教家庭中適應她的新生活。此書在 2003 年再版時換了新的封面。當初芙蘿珥‧畢蕾會寫下這個故事，的確是一個學生的遭遇讓她有感而發，該生因為抗爭不同的宗教理念，而被逐出家門。

到目前為止，芙蘿珥‧畢蕾已經為青少年寫了 13 本小說，每一本都讓人讀後低迴不已。難怪她是這麼一位對青少年具有強烈吸引力的作家。

請上網發現作家更多的吸引力：http://www.bookcouncil.org.nz/writers/bealefleur.html

馬丁・貝屯（Martin Baynton）

照中國人的算法，1953年出生的馬丁・貝屯（Martin Baynton）生肖屬蛇，也就是俗稱的「小龍」，一直到34歲的壯年期，他才從出生地英國倫敦移民到紐西蘭來定居。馬丁・貝屯是一位多才多藝的作家，不只是他寫書寫故事的對象有兒童也有成人，同時他還為舞台、電視和廣播寫劇本。他給孩子們寫書不光是提供文字而已，連插圖也不假他人之手，反倒是許多別人書上的插圖就出自「他手」；除了又寫又畫，馬丁・貝屯還會演，電視和劇院都成為他揮灑演技的舞台。

馬丁・貝屯最早受到影響的「啟蒙書」是麥爾先生（A・A・Milne）寫的《小熊維尼》（或稱維尼普普熊）（Winnie the Pooh）故事系列。從孩童時期就喜愛閱讀的一股動力，激勵他朝著「讀而優則寫」的方向走下去。「作家是我心目中的英雄」，他說。並且他認為當作家最精彩的部份就是作自己的老闆，雖然有時候這個沒有員工的老闆免不了會覺得寂寞。

畫插圖、寫故事豐富了馬丁・貝屯的生活。這位生肖屬「小龍」的作者，他的許多書都以飛龍和恐龍為特色，以下我們就要來看看，這兩種在中文裡都叫「龍」的動物，在他的書裡扮演著什麼樣的角色：

在馬丁‧貝屯居住的地方，對於金礦開墾的傳說眾說紛云，一直是一個有爭議性的話題，這就難怪他的書《山丘底下》(*Under the Hill*) 寓意深濃，有著含沙射影的教化意味。話說山丘底下有一個露天金礦，當這批採礦人魚貫而入⋯⋯

> 推土機，載土車，還有挖土器，又爆破又挖掘，連咒罵帶喘氣，他們挖到了一塊岩石，一塊原來藏得很隱密、穩若磐石的岩石，一塊蟄伏在山丘底下動也不動的岩石。⋯⋯這塊岩石很堅硬，又是個老頑固，它忠心耿耿地死守著寶貴的金礦。
>
> 於是他們只好從山丘上偷，一天偷一點，一點又一天，他們採得金礦，再把金子運走⋯⋯

結果那塊蟄伏在山丘底下動也不動的岩石，原來是一隻長得像迷你恐龍的動物。終於，這隻睡龍甦醒過來了，他可是在金子堆裡長大的，所以他的主食就是金子，自己守著的金子不能吃，他只好到處覓食找金子充飢。他也施展神偷大法，在人群裡尋尋覓覓，到處偷。他趁人睡覺的時候偷，他從那些探勘沉船的潛水者身上偷，他從教堂、從寺院裡偷，甚至從鑲牙的質材上偷，當然銀行更是要偷。總而言之，只要哪裡能找到金子，他都偷。

最後人們實在都受夠了。他們跟迷你龍商議，請他把偷去的金子還來。迷你龍也不是省油的燈，他說只要人們把他日漸虛空的山丘裡填滿金子，他就同意他們的要求。填座金山談何容易，人們想出了一個替代的方法，他們造了一個塑膠山丘，跟迷你龍達成協議。不過，這個故事有個很圓滿的結局，這隻迷

你龍把另一座山改造成一個美好的地方，上面覆蓋著一片金光燦燦的小黃花。

1988 年由紐西蘭學友公司（Scholastic New Zealand）發行的《珍妮與飛龍》（Jane and the Dragon）是一系列有強烈的女性主義傾向的少年小說，主人翁珍妮是一個騎士，她不喜歡女紅，雖然傳統上認為女孩子都應該對縫紉有興趣。她更不想成為一個「待字閨中」的少女，整天等著嫁個如意郎君，她只想作個騎士，但是：

> 她的父親聽到這話大笑了起來，「簡直胡說八道，」他說，「只有男孩子才能當騎士。」

珍妮不死心，她告訴每一個人她想要當騎士，可是所有聽到的人反應都一樣兒──大笑。唯一把她的話正經八百聽進去的是一個當弄臣的人，也就是在宮廷裡講笑話、取悅人的小丑，他有心幫助珍妮，要把她訓練成一個騎士。然後有一天，一隻飛龍偷走了王子。身穿騎士裝的珍妮，見狀衝出去救王子。她……

> 尾隨著飛龍來到他棲身的山穴。
> 「放開那個男孩！」她以她最嚴屬的聲音提出要求。
> 飛龍聞聲大笑了起來。

可想而知，隨後免不了一場爭戰。珍妮與飛龍彼此都有機會差一點就殺了對方，但是他們並沒有這樣做。當珍妮問飛龍為什麼他不殺了她，他回答說因為他不喜歡傷害人。

「那為什麼你要偷襲王子？」

「因為別人期待我這樣做。」

「那麼就做別人所不期待的。」珍妮的話中有話。

接下來珍妮向飛龍揭開她是女兒身的秘密，然後他倆結為好友。珍妮同意每星期六都去拜訪飛龍。當她帶著王子回到皇宮，雖然國王和皇后對她十分感激，但對這個陌生的騎士仍是感到神秘不解。等他們恍然大悟原來是珍妮女扮男裝，國王立刻用最大的榮耀來感謝珍妮，除了策封她為騎士，還允許她每週六都可以休假。

在 1990 年出版的續集《飛龍的目標》（The Dragon's Purpose）裡，珍妮，這位正牌的騎士，在她定期造訪的某個週六，發現飛龍一副可憐兮兮的樣子。追問之下，原來飛龍覺得自己的人生毫無目的，因為他再也嚇不倒人了。他愛星期六，這自然是沒話說，但星期裡的其他日子就乏味極了，他根本無事可做。珍妮非常憂心，她問她的朋友，那位宮廷裡的弄臣，該怎麼辦，但他也束手無策。珍妮轉向宮裡的巫師求助，但他正忙著編一個新的求雨咒，因為太久沒下雨了，就要鬧旱災是大事，所以也無暇顧及飛龍的小事。倒是後來珍妮想出了一個辦法——飛龍可以在萬聖節的遊行行列裡嚇人。這個主意不錯，可只是暫時有效，新鮮感一過，飛龍就說：

「……這真丟臉啊，小把戲而已。謝謝妳想盡辦法要幫助我，可是『搞笑』不是我生活的目的。」說完他就飛走了，連再見也沒說。

最後，飛龍「自力救濟」找到了解決問題的方法，而且不必嚇人，反而幫助了國王和全體人民。

「看我做的！」飛龍中氣十足地大聲吼叫。「我把雨從雲裡嚇出來了。天生我材必有用，我是一隻綠色的巨龍，是專門生來嚇雨雲的。」

馬丁・貝屯住在紐西蘭凡嘎瑪塔（Whangamata）的可樂曼德爾半島（Coromandel Peninsula）上，寫作是他生活的重心，騎馬是忙碌後的休閒活動。要知道更多有關他的消息，請上網站：http://www.bookcouncil.org.nz/writers/bayntonmartin.html

傑克・雷森比（Jack Lasenby）

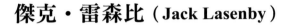

　　傑克・雷森比（Jack Lasenby）是一位榮獲兒童文學獎的作家，但這位作家原本從事的工作，與文學寫作並無關聯。大約在 1950 年代的時候，年輕的傑克雷森比縱橫在草原上、叢林中，以誘捕浣熊與追殺麋鹿為業，挖設陷阱，開槍射擊都是他的拿手好戲。然而，就像這個專欄裡所介紹的大多數作家一樣，傑克・雷森比「棄武從文」也教書去了，直到如今，來到位於首都的威靈頓教育學院，還看得到這位兒童文學家，在英文課上「春風化雨」的身影。

　　他的第一本小說，《湖泊》（The Lake），敘述一個十三歲的女孩的故事。主人翁露絲為逃避繼父的虐待，不惜離家出走，她一心奔向一個湖泊，因為父親去世前曾經帶她來這個湖邊度假。這是一個漫長的旅程，但是露絲從中獲得了力量和啟示。正如傑克雷森比其他的許多書一樣，所探討的主題往往是真情實境的，而主人翁的人生也常常是充滿挑戰的。

　　類似的情境在作者的另一本得獎作品中有跡可尋，只不過在這本名為《紅樹林的夏天》（The Mangrove Summer）的書裡，冒險竟然成為了災難。這本書的背景設在 1940 年代，傑克雷森比以自身孩童時期的經驗為藍本。童年時的他，每逢暑假就和三個表姐弟，在可樂曼都半島上的海灣一起度過。「因為我們的父親

和表姐弟家的母親都逝世了，所以一到夏天，我們就乾脆兩家併在一起，成立一個臨時的組合家庭。」作家解釋說。當時正是第二次世界大戰期間，故事中也安排了一段這群相濡以沫的表兄弟姐妹們，為逃避日本人的侵略，而躲進茂密的叢林裡的情節，之後故事有了一個悲劇性的轉折，在一場宴會熱鬧的當兒，兩個最小的弟弟居然失蹤了。

> 我們先找到德瑞克。雨已經下了一整晚。吉兒和格藍摸黑登上小艇，打算在黑暗中划船離去。我們在營地的灶爐上留下一鍋燉好的菜，然後沿著溪口的方向順流下去。當天光透亮的時候，我們的小舟也掠過那片沼澤地帶了。
>
> 又過了三條水道，安聽到了他的聲音。安跟我們的位置不同，她翻到小船的另一邊去，半游泳，半涉水，所以在我們還沒看到他之前，就先聽到聲音了。他，坐在紅樹林當中的一小塊乾地上，潮水已經淹到了腳。安聽到的正是他的啜泣聲，他已經喊不出來了。他甚至沒法舉起手臂……「吉米在哪兒？」安向他發問，順手摟了摟坐在船尾的德瑞克。
>
> 「那裡，」他的聲音像蚊子叫……「回那裡去。」他能說的就這麼多了。他好像神志不清到連我們都不認識了。

故事的場景遠離真實生活的就是作者在 1992 年出版的《魔法師》（The Conjuror），這部兒童讀物的確很引人注目，他引用了一個新潮又冷酷的社會，在那裡，社會的規範都是由眼睛的顏色來決定的；偏見、無知、殘忍與報復在作者的筆下一一可尋，但終究還是邪不勝正，一切無情的事跡，都在溫暖的友情裡得到了平衡……

　　傑克・雷森比的作品中，我最喜愛的是他的短篇故事集，《脫線舅舅》系列（the Uncle Trev series）以及《亨利的謊言》（The Lies of Harry Wakatipu）。說到 2001 年紐西蘭郵政兒童圖書獎的入圍名單，《亨利的謊言》也榜上有名，這可是實話，而且故事的場景也並非虛構，根據的就是作者自己的經驗，因為當年的他曾經是個逐鹿「草」原的好手。

　　我離家出走以後，就進了「殺鹿」戰場……在過去的時候，鹿可是叢林裡的一大害，於是政府出錢，請了少數幾個「心狠手辣」的傢伙來殺鹿。但是，事實也就到此為止了。接下來上場的亨利是一匹載負重物的馬。駄馬亨利很小氣，渾身發臭，而且還說謊……他能把謊言說成一個個異想天開的故事，不過他遇到了一個旗鼓相當的對手葳奇，葳奇是一隻很會說故事的狗。

　　「如今，」葳奇說，「小孩子都騎馬上學了。古早以前，我們是騎大象的。每個學校都有一個牧場，專門給象用的……」
　　「唬！」
　　「我家就有二十一個孩子。我們排成一列坐在我家大象的身上，而且還把我們的腳長長的伸出去……」
　　「唬！」
　　「我們家大象的名字叫葡萄牙……」
　　「唬！」
　　「亨利，我拜託你不要再『唬來唬去』了。我被你『唬』得簡直想不起我接下來要說什麼了。」
　　「唬！」

其實葳奇說謊的段數跟亨利一樣高超，不過她更高明的是處理家務，這可不是唬人的話。

第一本有關《愛飛姑姑》（Aunt Effie）的系列書，在 2002 年與讀者見面。這一連串別出心裁的故事再度以傑克·雷森比所鍾愛的地區為背景，那就是可樂曼都半島上的一大片森林。《愛飛姑姑》的系列書中，說到她六隻追豬的獵犬，和她二十六個姪兒姪女，與所有他們發生在森林裡的冒險故事，以及他們在海灣跟海盜展開的一場場戰役。

傑克·雷森比在寫作方面時常受到推崇，他曾經數度獲獎並得到研究獎金，在文壇的地位歷久彌新。這位勇於嚐新的作家宣稱他最喜歡的食物是，」凡地上爬的，天上飛的，到冰淇淋──」至於居住，則是離海越近越好，關於這點，住在威靈頓北端最高水位區的他是稱心如意的，在那兒，他可以駕著「世界上最美麗的小艇」揚帆出海。

想要知道傑克·雷森比更多的新鮮事，請上網梭巡：http://www.bookcouncil.org.nz/writers/lasenby.html

戴柏菈・本賽（Deborah Burnside）

安娜・麥肯姿（Anna Mackenzie）

瑪麗・貝羅（Mary Barrow）

艾德莉・布羅德本特（Adele Broadbent）

在「紐西蘭兒童文學的書與人」的一系列文章中，我們每次都以一位作家為主軸，為讀者勾勒出作家的樣貌，並且認識他的作品，了解他寫作的風格。專欄中，我們已經探討過多位得獎常勝軍的紐西蘭兒童文學作家，今天，換個角度，我們來看看四位冉冉上昇的明日之星，她們都以卓越的才能，為兒童文學這塊園地，注入一股活水般的新力量。

戴柏菈・本賽（Deborah Burnside）的第一本小說是《得意的一天》（On a Good Day），由紐西蘭最具國際聲譽的企鵝出版社（Penguin）於 2004 年出版。故事中的主人翁「李」有個酒鬼媽媽，他的爸爸則不知去向，是個謎樣的人物。這本小說十分有趣，以人物的刻劃取勝，套句電影用詞──叫「卡斯堅強」，也就是演員的陣容很有看頭，各個角色都擁有不可思議的個性。你瞧，那住在街對面的女孩「希」在「創意服裝大賽」裡大出風頭；住在隔壁的「艾薇」，從自己同樣「動盪不安」的生活裡，為「李」

提供了一個避難所。古娜，是李偷偷喜歡的對象，她不但外表超
「炫」，迷人的要死，而且還善解人意：

> 「李，」聽到我喊他，李的目光很快從我頭上掠過，盯住
> 我的膝蓋，又迅即落在他自己的胸前。「你知道當你在喪
> 禮上說到愛伯特的時候，我真的以你為榮……可是現在，
> 你說話兇巴巴，尖酸刻薄，一點也不像我昨天喜歡的那個
> 人。沒錯，你媽是犯了一個錯誤……」

多年來，戴柏菈就立定志向要當一個作家。雖然這是她第一
本長篇小說，但她已經寫了不少短篇故事，給大人或兒童看的都
有。她撰寫《得意的一天》得到紐西蘭作家協會「導師培訓計劃」
的基金贊助，她的導師正是我們曾經介紹過的資深作家泰莎‧杜
德（Tessa Duder）。

《高潮迭起》（High Tide）一書的作者是安娜‧麥肯姿（Anna
Mackenzie），學者出版社（Scholastic）在 2003 年發行，同年就
登上了兒童文學基金會的好書排行榜。書中的女主角珊曼莎報名
參加學校的健行之旅，可是讀者一打開書，就知道這趟旅行將會
「波濤洶湧」，因為小說一開頭就說：

> 假如我們早知道事情會發展成這樣，沒有人會爭先恐後地
> 踏上這趟旅程。但是「早知道……」這樣的後見之明說來
> 容易，誰都會說就會做的不一樣了。要不是我們有那點傻
> 勁，想要追求冒險，我猜什麼事都不會發生，可那──又
> 有什麼意思呢？

　　可是，事情還真是錯得離譜的可怕！這是一部「動作片」，一本充滿戲劇張力的小說。寫作的手法高超，故事的情節緊湊。「青少年在發掘自我，並發現屬於他們的世界。」作者安娜如是說。「他們在跟自己未曾有過的經驗打交道，從那些新的議題，新的情感中，找到可以長成大人的一條途徑。我樂於將這樣的前因後果，鋪陳在我的筆下。」有一位書評家論及《高潮迭起》時說：這本書「真的是一場驚悚的冒險之旅……實在是一本很好的小說。」

　　同樣以戶外活動為主題的則是另一本瑪麗・貝羅（Mary Barrow）寫的小說，書名為《又苦，又難，我受夠了》（Rough, Tough and Had Enough），由「學者」出版。我們進入書的世界裡與麥可相逢，看到他一副不甘願的樣子跟著爸爸去登山，他還在抗議，可是由不得他反對，路是越來越難走，家也越離越遠了。接著父子倆遇到一個獵人，一開始這個獵人態度蠻橫，對他們很不友善，不過麥可從他身上學到很多叢林求生的技巧，而且無意間也學到如何修正父子關係。後來，麥可的父親受傷了，這時野外常識豐富的麥可，不但奪得先機搶救了爸爸的性命，同時也讓那位獵人刮目相看，理所當然地贏得了他的敬佩與友誼。

　　作者瑪麗有一副觀察入微的好眼力，而且顯然對故事中的地勢場景十分熟悉。

　　她描述：就在一天的艱苦跋涉之後，麥可與父親來到了一個小茅舍，打算在那兒過夜……

　　　「我躺了下來，全身的筋骨總算可以放鬆了。四週靜悄悄的，只有奄奄一息的柴火還在嗶嗶、剝剝、嘶嘶，小屋裡安靜得好奇怪……就在我緊擁著溫暖、柔軟的睡袋快要睡

著的時候，我聽到外面開始下雨了。雨聽起來下得不大，輕輕柔柔的，好像催眠曲。我把身子更往睡袋裡縮，依偎著這個暖呼呼、毛茸茸的大蛹繭，期待著淅淅瀝瀝的雨聲送我進入夢鄉。然而，毫無預警地，夜空傳來霹靂雷響，大雨傾盆而下，豆大的雨珠猶如機關槍的子彈，掃射在鐵皮屋頂上……大風將屋頂拔起，沒有蓋子的小屋嚇得不住地戰慄，抖得好像就要發射到太空去了。」

艾德莉‧布羅德本特（Adele Broadbent）的作品《小傑克》（Wee Jack）大致上是根據她祖父的故事。十五歲的小傑克就要展開職業騎師的學徒生涯，他對此非常興奮。艾德莉為寫這部小說，徹底地作了番研究，首先要將馬場「走透透」。在一次冬日黎明前探訪賽馬場歸來，她說：去實地感受一下你所設的場景，去聞一聞，聽一聽，會讓你下筆時輕易許多。我不是騎師，但我想體會一下祖父的經驗……在那種沒有手套，圍巾或是帽子可以阻擋冷冽寒風的惡劣條件下……我走在啾啾的鳥鳴當中，與那些從我身旁掠過的沉沉馬蹄聲形成了對比……要是沒有經歷那個在賽馬場的清晨，我是不可能描繪出那些相關的種種情況。

我們就舉以下的例子，來看看艾德莉是如何把她的研究寫進她的小說中：

「世界上我最愛的事就是騎馬，而且要跑得很快。風呼呼地『刷』在我的臉上，我聽到馬蹄鏗鏗有聲、節奏分明地在我腿下『答答答』。我覺得自己成為那隻快馬的一部分。」

　　上述四位作家，都住在紐西蘭北島的霍克斯海灣，而且都是愛跟孩子說故事的媽媽，說還不夠，要用寫的，於是一本又一本她們的書登上市面，也希望愛書的讀者越來越多。

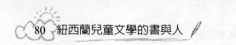

關達・騰內（Gwenda Turner 1947－2001）

澳洲是關達・騰內（Gwenda Turner）的出生地，說來她還是個中輟生，十六歲的時候就離開了學校，她投入職場的第一份工作是當秘書，秘書生涯三年後，她移民紐西蘭，又重新回到學校，在威靈頓技術學院選修「構圖設計」的課程，拿到這份很實用的文憑之後，她自己經營了一間手工藝品設計工作室，而且還兼差作繪圖設計的咨詢師，1974 年關達小姐成為騰內太太，從此以基督城為家。

關達・騰內為兒童書寫與插畫的第一本書在 1983 年出版，書名叫《樹女巫》（The Tree Witches）。這本書連續兩年為作者在不同國家帶來獲獎的肯定，1984 年贏得紐西蘭的羅梭插畫獎，次年又在澳洲成為 1985 年度最佳兒童圖畫書。從那以後，她出版了將近三十本書，所有的書都深獲小朋友的喜愛。

關達・騰內的作品風格是寫實派的，她以紐西蘭的真實情境作為故事的背景，書中的孩童都生活在典型的紐西蘭環境裡。「我的書寫作風就是要貼近生活，要表現生活的真實面」她說，「而且對我所畫的每一樣東西我都會下功夫研究。」除了故事書，她還是教材書的作者，那些具教學功能的書，如《紐西蘭 ABC》（New Zealand ABC）與「紐西蘭 123」（New Zealand 123），以及「在那遙遠的農莊」（Over on the Farm）和《農場上的動物》（Farm

Animals）都是由「企鵝」出版。「企鵝」出書，品質保證，不但富教育意義，而且也趣味盎然。

> 在那遙遠的農莊
> 是小魚潛水的地方
> 還住著一隻老母蛙
> 以及她的小蝌蚪
> 五隻
> 你們要游泳老母蛙說
> 我們在游泳小蝌蚪答
> 於是它們整天游泳
> 就在那小魚潛水的地方

　　如前面所說，關達‧騰內用文字表現出一本本的「寫真集」，她的書都是以現實生活為依據。她曾說：「我喜歡根據事實來寫故事，凡真正發生的事，我所遇見的小孩和動物，都可以成為我書中的情節和角色。我喜歡運用事實──「一個真正被記在心裡的時刻」。《建築工的貓》（The Builder's Cat），是又一本「企鵝」印行的書，書裡頭的貓是真有其貓，建築工「苦伯先生」也真有其人，這隻貓天天跟著苦伯去上工，更是真有其事。這隻叫「亞伯漢」的貓很喜歡到處去探險，他一會兒進了手推車，一會兒又爬上了樹，再過會兒又見他在水桶裡翻翻搞搞，要不在水罐裡撥撥弄弄。他不在乎，他一點也不在乎──那些圍繞著他的噪音，就像鑽孔機發出來的「嘰……」，或是苦伯的鐵錘敲出來的「鏗鏗鏗……」。

確實，關達的書不以情節取勝，故事性並不強，說來只是寫下了「一個真正被記在心裡的時刻」。像「企鵝」1998 年出版的《渡船》（The Ferry Ride），就是關於一個小男孩跟爸爸坐船出遊的興高采烈的一天。他們乘的船是連接南北島之間的渡輪，讀者跟著這對父子去觀看那些小車、大車——都被裝卸到了船上，他們看到船隻從碼頭開走，還一起數到底有幾隻海鷗一路跟著他們。海風吹呀吹的，把他們都吹餓了，於是父子倆進了餐廳，當他們吃起了熱騰騰的薯條，讀者也看得津津有味。然後，最棒的事出現了，他們在船橋上遇到船長，船長摘下自己的帽子戴在小男孩的頭上。

　　「爹地和我從船橋上看出去，視野實在太棒了！陸地，哇塞！」我大叫著說，「我們看到陸地了！」

　　我個人最愛的書是《便宜狗與口袋貓》（Penny and Pocket），敘述的是一隻流浪貓和一隻小家犬的故事。流浪貓很瘦小，小到可以放進口袋裡，所以得到「口袋」這個名字；母性十足的小家犬「便宜」，一看到「口袋」就喜歡她了。

　　「便宜」以為「口袋」是她的寶寶。她小心翼翼地把「口袋」銜在嘴裡，儼然一副貓媽媽的樣子。

　　關達・騰內於 2001 年離開了這個世界，但一本本她所寫、所畫的書依然伴隨著紐西蘭以及這個世界的兒童，這許許多多的好書，就是她為兒童文學留下的文化遺產。

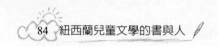

　　查詢更多相關訊息，可至以下網站：http://library.christchurch.
org.nz/Childrens/FamousNewZealanders/Gwenda.asp¶

寶拉・布客（Paula Boock）

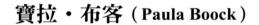

　　「寶拉・布客」（Paula Boock）是一位為青少年寫小說的兒童文學家，她所寫的作品是文學中的青少年。一般說來，兒童文學由於閱讀對象和寫作目的的不同，它的寫作方法、故事情節、主旨含意以及文體、文筆等，也會有其特別的要求與風格；因此，這類以青少年為主題的作品即是文學中的青少年。

　　紐西蘭南島中部的但尼丁，一個蘇格蘭氣息濃厚的城市，就是「寶拉・布客」生長的地方。奧塔哥大學畢業後，她在一位著名的出版業者手下擔任編輯，之後以亮眼的成績被另一家大型出版社網羅，而且在 1995 年的時候，成為該出版社的合夥人。

　　「寶拉・布客」編而優則寫，在她自己當老闆以前，就已經出版過好幾本書了，並且在 1991 與 1994 年分別獲得「創意紐西蘭」與「但尼丁教育學院」兩個文教單位的肯定。她的第一本小說——《出局》（Out Walked Mel）於 1992 年進入年度好書的決選，1994 年她的第二本小說登上了這個寶座。具有出版人身份的她，直到 1999 年才再次與獎結緣，接受了母校頒發的一項寫作研究獎。

　　《全壘打》（Home Run）是 1996 年兒童文學獎青少年類書中極受矚目的作品。書中的主人翁畢佩鞠是班上的新同學，她剛從基督城轉學到奧克蘭這所多元文化的學校，她覺得自己截然跟

周遭的環境格格不入。她唯一能交上朋友的是幾個在班上安安靜靜的女孩子，被別人稱作「軟腳蝦」的那幾位。但畢佩鞠不會那麼輕易認輸，她要跟大家打成一片。她知道有件事自己很拿手，可以成為眾人注目的焦點——那就是打壘球。她以前在基督城參加的球隊好幾次都拿到全區的冠軍呢。不過，就在要表現的時候，她卻好緊張……結果：

> 「突然，一切都太遲了，她知道大勢已去，那顆球就那樣眼睜睜地從她身旁咻地掠過，自動飛出了一個『全壘打』，落在外野那個公園的籬笆上。畢佩鞠簡直不能相信。她楞在原地……她從來沒有失手接過這麼簡單的球。」

人家那個團體，她還是插不進去。忽然靈機一動，她乾脆跟那幾個看不起她的，有樣學樣，她們不乖是吧？她也豁出去算了。

於是，事情果然變得更加棘手：

> 「商店的角落有一個牌子，上面寫著：順手牽羊者，立即送警法辦……。她發現有幾捲錄音帶是雪兒一直想要的，她握在手裡慢慢地往下移，移到架子下方的位置，然後再小心翼翼地見四下無人把帶子塞進書包裡……」

終於，跟阿塔的友情開始萌芽了，這段友誼很特殊，卻也帶來很多困擾，因為彼此的背景很不相稱。畢佩鞠來自一個富裕的家庭，阿塔則是窮人家的孩子。畢佩鞠是歐裔白人，阿塔是原住民毛利人。《全壘打》一書洋溢著作者「寶拉·布客」的典型風

格，有一個精力充沛、鬥志旺盛的女性主人翁，不偏離現實的場景以及與社會相關的情況。

另一本 1997 年寫的作品《不怕真相，勇於承諾》（Dare Truth or Promise），於 1998 年入圍紐西蘭郵政兒童文學獎。路易與葳莉在「大漢堡」打工的時候認識，可是兩人的生活卻大不相同。路易是學校裡的模範生，預備要唸大學以後當律師。

反之，葳莉被學校開除，她寄身在一個酒吧，打算將來作廚師，但她本本分分的，根本沒有指望路易會介入她的生活，並且改變了她的人生。

《亂世權王》（Power& Chaos）這本小說在千禧年登場。故事根據一部新潮的電視連續劇編寫的，內容都在預言「未來」。話說當病毒開始摧毀所有的紐西蘭成年人，馬丁的媽媽也受到攻擊，病得奄奄一息：

> 那個週末媽媽撐不下去了，她被送進了醫院。我不知道要如何寫下那個時刻，當時媽媽還在對我們笑，她一直想交代什麼，可是我只看到她臉上寫滿了——病毒。那麼多條的紋路，一雙空洞的眼睛，那張迅速凹陷的臉⋯⋯我們戴著醜醜的口罩站在旁邊看著她，心裡很清楚媽媽活著的時候不多了。

大多數的青少年小說都有個愉快的結局，但這本書不同於一般。這個故事告訴我們「權力使人墮落，絕對的權力使人墮落得更徹底。」馬丁心裡明白，所有的成年人都在病毒的侵害下垂死掙扎，年輕人可以當道掌權了。於是他變成這個新秩序中的領導者——一個眼露凶光，冷酷無情的「亂世權王」。

　　從寫書到編輯連出版，都可以一貫作業的「寶拉・布客」住在首都威靈頓，目前以寫電視劇本居多。歡迎登入她的網頁：http://www.bookcouncil.org.nz/writers/boock.html¶

真妮絲・麥瑞兒特（Janice Marriott）

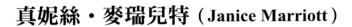

　　紐西蘭北島的東部區延伸入太平洋，是全世界最早看到日出的非島嶼地區，那兒的每座小鎮都可看到毛利文化，其中最大的城市就叫作「吉斯本」（Gisborne）。

　　沿著東岸往下走，會來到以陽光充沛的氣候、美麗的海灘、風平浪靜的海岸以及歷史悠久的葡萄園而聞名的霍克斯灣區，該地區的主要城市「內皮爾」（Napier）被稱為裝飾藝術之都，是世界上裝飾藝術最集中的地方。

　　真妮絲・麥瑞兒特（Janice Marriott）的中學教育就是在「吉斯本」與「內皮爾」兩處完成的。說來真妮絲・麥瑞兒特的家庭善於遷徙，她十一歲的時候，隨家人從出生地英國移民來紐西蘭，然後居住過上述兩個城市之後，她又前往首都去念維多利亞大學，並於畢業後留在威靈頓擔任圖書館員。然而求新求變的她接下來遠渡重洋去美國和加拿大，並涉足傳播界，她在廣播及電視公司工作數年。之後，再度回到紐西蘭，這回她進了教育界當老師，而且從 1980 年代開始為兒童寫作。1994 年她成為奧克蘭大學首屆的駐校作家。

　　真妮絲・麥瑞兒特的小說十分寫實而且大多數都很幽默。不過《十字路》（Crossroads）是一個例外。這本為青少年寫的小說主題較為嚴肅，探討死亡與其帶來的哀痛。它贏得了 1996 年

少年小說的首獎，被評論為「藉由隱喻及文學的共鳴，特別是來自莎翁戲劇《哈姆雷特》中的回響，深切刻劃兩個少年在緊要關頭所面臨的問題，探討的手法令人激賞。」作家本人則輕描淡寫地說，這本小說是有關「做一個駕駛者應該擔負的責任」。

「我寫，」真妮絲說，「關於孩子們是多麼難以了解成人世界的有趣故事。」1993 年由「學者」（Scholastic）出版的《「篩」腦筋》（Brain Drain）就是這樣的一本書。書中的主人翁是亨利，亨利的母親告訴他，她想要賣掉他們住的房子。當時亨利正無精打采地看著電視：

> 「有位政壇人士告訴我們，去年有兩萬伍仟人從紐西蘭移民到國外，相當於一個「提瑪魯」鎮的人口，換句話說，好比一個小鎮就不見了⋯⋯損失的可都是我們年輕人中的精英分子。」這位人士稱此現象為「『篩』腦筋」。一聽播報員說完這話，我精神一振，坐直了身子。
>
> 「什麼叫『篩』腦筋？」
>
> 「噢，好腦筋的年輕人都走了，這不是『篩腦筋』嗎？而且是『汰新換舊』，把好的新的都篩選掉了；留下來的都是老的不好的。」亨利的媽媽回答說。
>
> 「可⋯⋯可是，妳以前為什麼沒告訴我呢！」
>
> 我從來不了解原來國家也像衣服一樣──有新穎的也有過時的──
>
> 我衝回我的房間，每逢有關鍵問題要處理的時候，它的功能就會加倍──成為我的辦公室。腦筋不夠靈光的人聽了這個消息會陷入沒來由的恐慌，但我有企業家的頭腦，具備應對的能力。我把握當下的問題⋯⋯然後再假設未來的

情境。這叫做事先計劃……我忽然領悟到只有這個別出心裁的計劃才能夠解決我目前生活中的問題……我無法阻止媽媽賣房子，但我可以不必待在這兒上街頭鬼混。我可以移民！我可以加入那個「篩腦筋」計劃。

只是還有一個小問題。亨利可得籌到買飛機票的錢。然而這個移民加籌錢的一大一小兩個問題，都需要亨利在一個月內搞定。《篩腦筋》全系列有三部曲。另兩本同樣繞著這個搞笑的亨利打轉的書分別是：1989 年出版的《給黎司理的信》（Letters to Lesley）以及 1997 年的《與魚共吻》（Kissing Fish）。

「我喜歡寫平常日子裡的不平常的事情，」真妮絲‧麥瑞兒特（Janice Marriott）如是說。「我喜歡透過好奇的眼睛去觀看這個世界，就像一個純真的小孩一樣。我喜歡孩子們旺盛的精力和他們的幽默感，這些也正是我注入寫作的東西。」

她的一本我個人最喜愛的作品，《霍譜的彩虹》（Hope's Rainbow），就囊括了上述所有特點，成為作者詮釋這段話最典型的範例。

霍譜這個名字的含意是希望。當霍譜的媽媽帶著她和哥哥弟弟……離開爸爸……住到城裡，霍譜的生活有了一個大轉變。而這一切都因為父母倆，為了請獸醫的意見不合大吵了一架，就分開來住了。霍譜簡直不懂大人是怎麼回事。但她可知道自己討厭住在城裡，也不喜歡要擔負起照顧弟弟的責任。她想念老家的羊，更懷念鄉村的生活，而且她還要替狗狗布森操心。布森跟她一樣，過慣了鄉下日子，也不適應城市的生活。可是以上這些都不算最糟的，她其實最擔心媽媽，媽媽整天除了坐在電視前發獸對什麼都沒興趣，以往的活力全不見了。霍譜決定設法讓媽媽快

樂起來，她為媽媽的生日籌劃了一個驚喜派對，但是一場突發的小火災又干擾了她的計劃，結果，皇天不負苦心人，霍譜得到了一場比她期望的更要好的派對。

真妮絲・麥瑞而特目前定居在威靈頓。她家有一個豪華氣派的大花園，景色美不勝收。能夠經營這樣一座頂級的花園，是需要專業的功力的，這就難怪「葉茨兒童園藝叢書」（Yates Gardening for Kids series）會邀請真妮絲為他們寫一系列以園藝為主題的兒童書。於是《為小朋友寫的園藝書》（Gardening for Kids）在 2002 年堂堂上市，並且配上艾琳娜・裴陀芙（Elena Petrov）的插畫，讓這本提供豐富園藝知識的童書，在圖書界大放異彩。

次年，同樣由艾琳娜・裴陀芙所繪的第二本書問世，插圖依然精美的叫人愛不釋手，內容卻截然有別，這本名為《自己種來吃》（Growing Things to Eat）的園藝書，教小朋友如何創造出一個生機盎然的菜園，以及製作稻草人的方法等等。讓他們在接觸到第一本書中所提到的有關土壤、花樹與鳥類的知識後，再進一步學習落實在生活中的實務操作。不僅如此，作者還在書中告訴小讀者許多有趣的例子：如何讓自己的名字長在所種植的南瓜上，又如何在寬口瓶裡栽種小黃瓜；或即使沒有園地，作家也能教你怎樣培育你自己的食物。看來有綠手指的真妮絲・麥瑞兒特，的確能夠「點石成金」呢。

歡迎參觀真妮絲・麥瑞而特的網站：http://www.bookcouncil. org.nz/writers/marriott.html

隆恩‧貝肯（Ron Bacon 1924－2005）

　　隆恩‧貝肯（Ron Bacon）不但名列紐西蘭最資深的兒童文學家之一，而且論敬老尊賢也絕對有資格。1924 年誕生於澳洲，七歲的時候隨家人移民到紐西蘭，然後跟很多我們這一系列介紹過的作家一樣，他先是踏上教書之途，然後在教學相長中，他看到兒童讀物中有所欠缺的地方，那就是有關毛利文化的眾多傳說，在紐西蘭的英語兒童文學裡，居然還是一片未經耕耘的園地。

　　我們或許知道，紐西蘭是十八世紀晚期，歐洲人發現的一塊海中新地，而島嶼上的原住民就叫作毛利人，而且如今根據 DNA 的比對，毛利人與我們的高山同胞很有淵源，據說就是一千多年前從亞洲這邊一路漂流下去到紐西蘭的。話說回來，英國政府在 1840 年正式將紐西蘭納為英國的殖民地，當然不但帶來了純白的綿羊，歐裔的白種人也捎來了純白的英國文化，所以在二十世紀初期，紐西蘭政府是不鼓勵原住民說他們的母語的，學校裡教的當然都是英國的傳統語文，其實毛利人有許多有趣的傳說與文化的精髓，都值得讓小朋友了解，卻缺乏用英文寫給兒童看的素材，於是當年的隆恩老師，以他的健筆，在「復興毛利文化」這件有意義的事上，立下了一個領先的地位。

　　他的第一本書叫作《男孩與怪物》（The Boy and the Taniwha），出版於 1966 年，是後來許多同類型書中的鼻祖，當

時還請到一位著名的毛利畫家兼彫刻家「跨刀演出」，書中所有的插畫，都由這名叫「帕拉・瑪曲提」（Para Matchitt）的藝術家提供。之後隆恩又根據民間傳說繼續創作出《神人與女鳥人》（Hautupatu and the Bird Woman ---1979），《民族之家》（The House of the People--- 1977），以及《祖先的大魚》（The Fish of Our Fathers--- 1984），並且以有關——紐西蘭北島是當年一個半神人所釣到的大魚……的這部作品，在 1985 年贏得了最佳圖文書獎。

　　在這一系列傳說故事中，最「出色」的一部就屬再次由毛利藝術家「帕拉瑪曲提」配合插畫的《盧亞與討海人》（Rua and the Sea people---1968）。書中的主人翁盧亞是一個毛利小男孩，跟祖母住在海邊的一個小村莊，盧亞每天看海，越看越覺得海水晶瑩閃耀，波光粼粼的海域，就像在暖暖的夏日夜晚，天空中閃閃發亮的一片星海。看海的日子裡，盧亞最愛看漁人們擺動著他們的船槳，將獨木舟划進港灣。盧亞一天天長大，他也學會了所有這些討海人的招式——如何上魚餌，如何成為一個會跳毛利戰舞的勇士等。直到有一天，海港不再平靜，已經長成為一個勇士的盧亞，與族人一起出海，要將入侵者——那金髮碧眼、長相和他們不一樣的「仙人」……趕出去。迎戰的結果，「仙人」並沒有傷害盧亞，還給了盧亞一根釘子——一個看起來好像很有用的東西。故事到此你大概已經猜到了，那金髮碧眼的當然不是仙人，他們就是第一批從海路踏上紐西蘭，開始與土著以物易物的歐洲人。

　　這本書另一個值得一提的就是它的插畫，全都是印象派的，所有的圖片都由幾何圖形組成，方型三角型，就像彫刻的一樣。畫家解釋說：早期的毛利人沒有文字，他們記錄下故事的方法，就是透過彫刻或繪圖，要不就連編織，都可以述說一個故事。表

現出來的圖樣——有的彎曲如一捲捲綻放的蕨草，有的則線條流暢好比層層起伏的波浪。

隆恩當然不只是寫有關古老的傳說，他也兼顧現代生活中的故事，正如他的一系列以「荷米」為主角的書。其中《荷米，他的滑板與他的偶像》（Hemi, the Skateboard and Susquatch Harrison---1992）是我最愛的一本，該書的插畫者是理查・候特（Richard Hoit）。荷米的這塊滑板很有來頭，是他舅舅從香港帶來送他的。書中描述說：

> 這塊滑板的顏色十分搶眼，鮮艷的翠綠和亮麗的粉紅，與同樣粉色的輪子頗為相稱，造型也很不錯，有個彎彎翹起的尾端。另外配套的安全帽也是粉紅色的，附帶的包包裡還有短襪，護膝和護肘。

學校的網球場是練習滑板的最佳場地，當荷米去的時候，已經有人捷足先登了，而且這人還吸引了大批孩童圍觀，他就是大家都知道的滑板好手——韓瑞森，正在表演他拿手的滑板倒立。可是等荷米的滑板在眾人的眼前一出現，許多小朋友都湊上來了，圍著他的新滑板問東問西，眼光裡充滿了羨慕，這時韓瑞森也加入了。

> 韓瑞森盯著那塊板子，然後慢慢地，輕輕地，他撫摸著那塊滑板，並且用臉去摩娑，感受一下那板子的光滑。「酷，真酷啊！」他說。荷米覺得很好，因為他知道這絕不是韓瑞森平常會對小孩子說話的方式。
> 韓瑞森試滑了一下荷米的滑板，他一旋身，示範了好幾個

高難度的動作。

荷米開心得笑了，他用腳踩住板子，正準備要滑的時候他
說：「酷啊！真是太酷了！」

書後還附上「兒童使用滑板須知」，增加了本書的實用性。

隆恩·貝肯寫過的書不計其數，其中有本在 1999 年紐西蘭
郵政兒童書獎的「非故事」類別中入圍。這本極為有意思的作品，
由馬努·史密斯（Manu Smith）插畫，書名是《給土地命名》（The
Naming of the Land），內容關於各個毛利文地名的名稱與意義，
以及名稱背後的古老故事，並且說到當初給許多地方命名的一位
牧師的智慧。這是一本參考價值很高的書。另外一本在 2003 年
再度入圍的則是《衝浪救生》（Surf Lifesaving），這本書裡穿插的
全是相片，由安森尼·西斯（Anthony Heath）攝影。

隆恩·貝肯的寫作生涯十分漫長，但一直與現實接軌得很
好，雖然年高德劭的隆恩爺爺已於 2005 年因癌症去世，然而至
今仍有五十多本書不斷再版。1994 年，他曾榮膺一個極高尊崇地
位的服務獎，為了表彰他為紐西蘭兒童文學所付出的——長期又
卓越的貢獻。

歡迎至隆恩·貝肯的網頁：http://www.bookcouncil.org.nz/
writers/baconron.html

後記

創意與想像齊放的文學盛宴

——紐西蘭郵政書獎

　　2005 年 5 月，紐西蘭舉辦了一場全國性的盛會，慶祝紐西蘭郵政書獎，特別是針對兒童與青少年的獎項。慶典的內容琳琅滿目，有閱讀，作家演講，網上機智測驗，人面彩繪等，甚至一些更加動態的，例如製作風箏以及放風箏大賽，還有集體創作海灘壁畫等活動，提供了許多小朋友可以動手參與的機會。在 2005 年紐西蘭郵政書獎當中，其間進入決選的好幾位作家，都是我們在這個專欄裡曾經討論過的，我想不如就用這個題材來個「溫故知新」，為這一系列文章劃上句點，現就介紹我們的「老朋友」出場。

　　說來，「薑還是老的辣」，大膽探究青少年問題的小說家——大衛‧西爾（David Hill）又以《返回》（Coming Back），一本涉及青少年飆車與車禍的小說，再次榜上有名。至於那位從多角度寫作的兒童小說家——肯恩‧凱特倫（Ken Catran），則以一個軍人的故事與大衛並駕其驅，這本小說的主人翁是個曾經參加第二次世界大戰的軍人，書名就是他的稱謂《二等兵——羅伯‧摩輪》（Robert Moran——Private）。接下來在少年小說領域受到矚目的，是以青少年主題為創作核心的——芙蘿珥‧畢蕾（Fleur

Beale），她有兩部作品獲得評審的青睞，一是《大地新歌》（A New Song in the Land），背景設在 1840 年，故事從我們的主角——一個毛利少年——逃離他的奴隸生涯起展開序幕。另一本叫《瀟灑走一回》（Walking Lightly）的，則風格迥異；描述一個富家女孩，雖然物質上不虞匱乏，父母又疼她，要什麼有什麼，但她就是沒興趣過這種養尊處優的生活，卻寧願選擇自食其力的方式去「追風逐月」，邁向世界。再來看圖文書的部份，那位既能寫又能畫的作家蓋文・畢夏普（Gavin Bishop），這次同樣發揮了他「出入傳統與現代」的特色，在《馴服太陽》（Taming the Sun）一書的四個毛利神話中，以取材自傳說又極具現代感的插圖取勝。

郵政書獎是分門別類頒發的。針對年齡層較低的少年小說類，2005 年奪得冠軍的是傑克・雷森比（Jack Lasenby）連同他的新書《愛飛姑姑與那座下沉的島》（Aunt Effie and the Island that Sank）。這「愛飛姑姑」系列書中的第三本，其實跟前兩冊一樣瘋狂。愛飛姑姑一刻也閒不下來。這回她和她二十六個姪兒姪女，又要繼續展開他們的尋寶之旅。有別於以前的是，這次他們走的是水路，而且要穿越海盜經常出沒的大海灣。真是緊張！精彩又刺激！難怪會得首獎。

除了評審團頒發的獎項之外，主辦單位還有一個「讀者票選獎」，由小朋友自己來決定——這個年度最受歡迎的兒童書，該獎落誰家。2005 年的得主正是我們介紹過的熟面孔：林俐・達德（Lynley Dodd）。對「紐西蘭的人氣繪本作家」這樣的稱號，林俐・達德當之無愧，這位能寫善畫的一把好手，多年來廣受歡迎的程度絲毫未減，如今再度以她「雙棲」的本領，創作出「另一艘方舟」（The Other Ark, 2004 年出版），與聖經中著名的「挪

亞方舟」媲美。故事中說到，當挪亞方舟已經收拾妥當正準備啟航，這時還有許多動物有待救援，於是有個叫山姆的，心一軟走不了了，他打算再裝滿一艘船才離開，可是當山姆開始連哄帶騙，勸誘那些如恐龍之類的珍禽異獸登船時，他才知道自己面臨的是一個多麼艱巨的任務……。

詩人葛瑞格理・歐布來恩（Gregory O'Brien）贏得了非小說類的首獎，得獎作品是：《南海》：為青少年介紹紐西蘭的現代美術（South Seas: Contemporary New Zealand Art For young People），該書筆調生動地將紐西蘭現代美術的來龍去脈娓娓道來，也教導青少年如何看待藝術。書中討論到的藝術家有 45 位，並且每位至少有一件作品被提出來作為範例。這本書就以這樣的方式，將過去三十年紐西蘭美術的發展具體而微地呈現在讀者面前。

相對於大多數受獎項肯定的作家，2005 年少年小說的頭獎得主伯納德・貝克特（Bernard Beckett），堪稱是個新人。他的得獎作品《男生女生，配！》（Malcolm and Juliet），被譽為是一本妙不可言，卻也非常具有爭議性的小說。書中的男主角馬空僅十六歲，有著一副科學家的好頭腦，然而卻人小鬼大，他決定要在那年的科學大展中，製作一部有關「性」的紀錄片參展。

2005 年郵政獎的總贏家：凱特・德・勾弟（Kate De Goldi），同時以《社團：樂莉的故事》（Clubs: A Lolly Leopold Story）一書在圖文書的類別中奪魁。話說樂莉的老師，羅芙小姐是個精彩的人物，她身上貼著大蜥蜴的圖騰，腦勺後的馬尾像圈套般地甩來甩去。幾乎她全班的學生都加入了至少一兩個社團，每個社團都有它自己的規則，但是樂莉老是漫不經心。後來羅芙老師答應樂莉，假如她能在各個社團前說故事，她就要在祖親會（註）會那天吹奏小喇叭。

　　以下是評審給予的評語：這本書介紹出一種新的寫作形式，正如著名的兒童文學家瑪格麗特·梅喜（Margeret Mahy）所說的，是紐西蘭兒童圖書界的一大突破。不在已熟悉的範疇中探索，是本書獲獎的最大原因。以多樣新鮮的手法來說故事，用圖片，或將文字與圖畫以各樣新穎的方式融合在一起，都成為本書的獨到之處。繪圖的逼真與語氣的真實，讓書中的場景栩栩如生，人物也呼之欲出。

　　隨著 2005 年郵政書獎的落幕，我們期待紐西蘭的兒童文學有更豐收的下一年。在這個尾聲響起的時刻，我更希望你有機會閱讀到此系列中提到的某些作品，與紐西蘭的讀者一起分享這些帶給他們極大樂趣的文字與插畫。

　　最後，提供一個網站，以便查詢更多有關紐西蘭郵政書獎的訊息：http://christchurchcitylibraries.com/Kids/LiteraryPrizes/NZPost/

註：祖親會是邀請祖父母參加的家長會。

附錄一

「第五屆世華大會」紐西蘭作家協會總會長
──威廉‧泰勒 William Taylor
「反映多元文化的紐西蘭」致詞摘要
New Zealand Writing and Writers
──A Reflection of Many Cultures

2003 年 3 月

1. 感謝這項與會的邀請。大洋洲華文作家協會與紐西蘭作家協會已締結友會盟約,從不同的文化語言中「異中求同」一直是兩會努力的目標,今日我會的受邀更是在這項合作上邁進了一大步。各位從世界各地前來共赴盛會,如此的規模與「壯舉」,令人印象深刻,我要代表紐西蘭作家協會向大會與各位表示由衷的感佩。

2. 如我在 2001 年簽署姐妹會協約的大會上所言,不論我們用何種文字寫作,我們分享的文學理念是一樣的,對人性的關懷是相同的,在此就不再贅言。

3. 紐西蘭的作品反映了多元文化,除卻英國殖民地色彩和全球文風的影響,更有特色的是我們的毛利文化。早期從歐洲移民來的先人不乏文字工作者,而本地的毛利原住民特別擅長

傳統文化與典故的口耳相傳，這些都反映在我們早期的英裔文學當中。今日的紐西蘭，不再以歐洲為中心，我們的移民來自四面八方，如許多亞洲民族的遷入；尤其是從早先到現今的華人，更是為我們的社會帶來不尋常的意義。早年我從事教育工作的時候，教過不少華裔子弟，如今有愈來愈多的華人來自香港、中國大陸與台灣。

4. 因此，我們的文學本質勢必隨著時代而改變。紐西蘭的國寶級作家「凱瑟琳・曼思菲爾」（Katherine Mansfield）於 1920 年代所寫的作品中總不脫先入為主的英國式的偏見。然而約半世紀後，一位獲得英國布克（Booker）文學大獎的紐西蘭作家——凱蕊・何眉（Keri Hulme），在她的得獎作品《先人》（The Bone People）之中幾乎已找不到這樣偏頗的痕跡。另一位少數碩果僅存的祖母級作家——「珍妮特・芙蘭」（Janet Frame），其作品則兼具以上兩種特質！小說界我們的前輩作家還有：茅里斯・吉（Maurice Gee），費歐娜・基嫚（Fiona Kidman），西開・思帖德（C K Stead）等等。毛利作家中著名的則有：派翠西亞・格蕾絲（Patricia Grace），河內・陶法瑞（Hone Tauwhare）以及威堤・依希瑪耶拉（Witi Ihimaera），他們都在筆下反映出毛利與歐裔白人的兩種文化。我們的詩人和劇作家以及寫非小說類型作家的觀點都不約而同，而且還更有世界觀。我們被翻成其他歐洲語言的書不在少數，可是譯成中文的卻十分罕見。2002 年在上海出版的「剩」賢奇蹟（Oracles and Miracles），由石帝文・愛爾德瑞德－格利格（Stevan Eldred-Grigg）所著，石莉安（Annie Shih）翻譯，聽說是第一本中文版的紐西蘭當代長篇小說。在文化的地圖上，紐西蘭地點雖小但發展蓬勃，並且日見獨特。在此我所

指的不僅是文學，而是包括各樣的藝術，如影片等。紐西蘭人在藝術方面所練就的本事，相對於在運動上苦練出的成果，可說是等量齊觀的。

5. 我們兒童文學「旅遊」的版圖則甚為寬廣。本人正是在兒童文學園地孜孜筆耕的一員。在此提出幾位作品時常跨國越界的知名人士，如：瑪格麗特‧梅喜（Margaret Mahy），裘依‧柯莉（Joy Cowley），林俐‧達德（Lynley Dodd）等，不勝枚舉；詳情請參閱台灣國語日報的〈紐西蘭兒童文學的書與人〉，這個專欄由紐西蘭作家協會前任總會長——瓊安‧羅吉兒－瓊思（Joan Rosier-Jones）撰寫。

6. 如前所述，如何進一步發展紐西蘭作家協會（NZSA）與大洋洲華文作家協會（OCWA）相輔相成的友好關係，是貴我兩會責無旁貸的目標，大洋洲會長翁寬先生對此極力促成，眾會員的同心協力亦功不可沒。基督城華文作協將華文文學與作家帶入紐西蘭文學展（Books and Beyond Festival）是一個好的開始，不僅應該延續下去，而且我們還可開創更多發展的方向。基督城華文作協的石莉安也是紐西蘭作協的榮譽會員，我個人也注意到她在華紐文學交流上所作的努力，Annie 與 Stevan Eledred-Grigg（石帝文）接續合作的〈紐西蘭文學史〉，已經在台灣的《明道文藝》連載；她同時也為 Joan Rosier-Jones（羅瓊安）英文原作的兒童文學專欄執筆，曾譯寫過一篇有關我的文章——〈反映童心，寓教於樂的威廉‧泰勒 William Taylor〉，文中提到我一本在國內外都得過獎的少年小說《綿羊艾格麗絲》（Agnes the Sheep），我雖不懂中文，但看到配合文章刊出的圖片和附帶的英文原名，也感受到被介紹的光榮與樂

趣。我必須承認，目前紐西蘭作家與圖書當局尚未廣泛注意到華文寫作在紐西蘭的現況，交流的重心比較偏倚在貴方，這點使我思之汗顏，希望能爭取改善。有此缺憾其實也是語言的問題，我方人士幾乎不識中文，其實我們也希望能了解你們的作品，這樣的交流才是對等之策。（譯者註：中華民國國際筆會的文學季刊——The Chinese Pen，就致力於將華文作品譯為英文，已代訂筆會季刊給紐西蘭作協。）

7. 再來談談我會的概況。紐西蘭作協的會員幾乎都是職業作家，全紐有六大分會，都定期開會聯誼。我們在各自寫作的時候是寂寞的，這樣的聚會則有助於我們脫離孤獨。當然交誼不是我們唯一的目的，更重要的是我們要為文學代言，跟政府與藝術基金單位——如「創意紐西蘭」（Creative New Zealand）為作家謀求更多的福利。換言之，我們在經營一個寫作的事業。NZSA 同時隸屬於國際筆會，也就是 International Pen，我們既是一個國際的組織，就更不該有任何地域的圍限。總之，不論我們從哪裡來，說何種語言，認同什麼文化，我們都面對一個「異曲同工」的事實，那就是——寫作！寫作使我們心手相連，文學藝術讓我們分享共通的喜怒哀樂與人生經驗。

8. 紐西蘭是一個多元文化投影的國家，而且變化日益多端。在紐西蘭的華文作家，為我們的社會增添了豐富的內涵與多方的樣貌。在此祝福你我作家耕耘的園地都枝繁葉茂，但仍不得不一吐苦水，寫作實在不是一件錢財豐收之事！往往寫作者還需兼顧自己營生的行業，在紐西蘭確實如此，別處呢？就教於各位。

9.　向大家請教學習之外，我也很樂意回答各位的問題。我帶來一些紐西蘭作家的書籍，其中也包括我自己的兩三本，敬請指教。非常感謝大會的熱忱安排與招待，也特別謝謝翻譯。這次台灣行的美好回憶將銘記我心，永誌難忘。再次，讓我用毛利語重複我的感謝：Tena koutou，tena koutou，kia ora koutou katoa

石莉安　節譯（Summarized and translated by Annie）

附錄二

紐西蘭作家協會與大洋洲華文作家協會
締結姐妹會協議書

2001 年 9 月

[宗旨]

　　在一個多元文化的世界裡，文學應該是無國界藩籬的。多年以來，英語一直是世界上最廣為流傳的語言，亦為最多人口所應用的外語。如今華語，在數量方面，亦有其獨步世界的地位，成為世上最多人口使用的語言。然而，因為華語在西方世界尚未普及，以至於中國人的內涵，那豐富的精神領域，未能讓許多西方人士一窺堂奧；相對地，紐西蘭由於地處偏遠的海角一隅，又屬年輕的新興國家，以至於紐西蘭文學未能如英美文學般地，廣為華文世界所認知，也是不爭的事實。文學與藝術，既然是人類表達情感最獨特，最細膩與精緻的方式，我們期待有著共同地緣的大洋洲華文作協與紐西蘭作協，能相互支持，幫助對方突破文化和語言的障礙，以達成雙方在彼此文化的東西方社會裡，獲得更多的尊重與接受。

　　以上的理想是有具體而微的模式的。在華作的分會「基督城華文作協」與紐西蘭作協的南島分會「坎特伯里作協」兩造之間就有良好的互動前例。「基督城華文作協」自 2000 年起在「坎

特伯里作協」的推薦之下，兩度受邀參與基督城「Books and Beyond」文學展，開創了外語文學進駐本地文壇的首例；同時，藉由該會所舉辦的「當西方遇上東方」翻譯講座的推動，促成了一本紐西蘭的英語小說即將於 2002 年在中國大陸出版中譯本的事實。

　　我們，同為寫作之人，分享著相同的理念。作為一個喜愛文學，又愛好和平者，我們更當致力於：將彼此的文學世界發揚光大，讓華語文提昇至英語文所受重視的同等地位，使紐西蘭文學擺脫地緣的侷限，以寬容的態度促進東西方文化更深層的了解，此等境界任重道遠，願共勉之。

[目標]

　　簡述如下（中英文若有出入，以英文為準。）
1. 雙方互為彼此協會之榮譽會員。
2. 兩會將促進介紹彼方的作者與作品。
3. 雙方將力圖促進「文化跨越」，以達成相互的欣賞與了解。
4. 加強雙方的交流，無論是文化、文學，或任何有關友誼聯繫的各項活動，有知會對方的義務，並協助對方取得參加的權益，希冀能從異中求同，在文學的基礎上，成就大同的理想。

　　以上所書之宗旨與目標，兩會可視實際情況之需要，加以潤飾或修改。兩會各推代表共同簽署此一文件，就此展開彼此的同伴關係，並表示全然支持「紐西蘭作家協會」與「大洋洲華文作家協會」締結為姐妹會。

紐西蘭作家協會（又名紐西蘭國際筆會）代表：
William Taylor（威廉‧泰勒）

大洋洲華文作家協會　代表：翁寬

協議書撰寫者：Dr Stevan Eldred-Grigg
（石帝文‧愛爾德瑞德－格利格　博士）
譯寫者：石莉安（Annie Shih）
註：在紐西蘭英文中，Dr＝Dr.；Mr＝Mr.

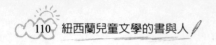

附錄三

紐西蘭兒童文學郵政書獎
（2005－2009 得獎名單）
New Zealand Post Book Awards
for Children and Young Adults

http://christchurchcitylibraries.com/Kids/LiteraryPrizes/NZPost

- 年度最佳書獎

2009	The 10 PM Questions— Kate De Goldi
2008	Snake and Lizard—Joy Cowley (illustrated by Gavin Bishop)
2007	Illustrated History of the South Pacific—Marcia Stenson (non-fiction winner)
2006	Hunter —Joy Cowley (junior fiction winner)
2005	Clubs: A Lolly Leopold Story —Kate De Goldi, ifflustrated by Jacqui Colley

- 小讀者票選獎

2009	The Were-Nana—Melinda Szymanik & Sarah Nelisiwe Anderson
2008	The King's Bubbles—Ruth Paul (the 2nd in 2008 NZ Post Picture Book)
2007	Kiss! Kiss! Yuck! Yuck! —Kyle Mewburn, Ali Teo & John O'Reilly
2006	Nobody's Dog —Jennifer Beck & Lindy Fisher
2005	The Other Ark —Lynley Dodd

- **兒童小說類**

2009	Old Drumble — Jack Lasenby
2008	Snake and Lizard—Joy Cowley
2007	Thor's Tale: Endurance and Adventure in the Southern Ocean —Janice Marriott
2006	Hunter—Joy Cowley
2005	Aunt Effie and Island that Sank —Jack Lasenby

- **青少年小說類**

2009	The 10 PM Questions—Kate De Goldi
2008	Salt— Maurice Gee
2007	Genesis —Bernard Beckett
2006	With Lots of Love from Georgia—Brigid Lowry
2005	Malcolm and Juliet —Bernard Beckett

- **非小說類**

2009	Back & Beyond: New Zealand Painting for the Young and Curious—Gregory O'Brien
2008	Which New Zealand Spider —Andrew Crowe
2007	Illustrated History of the South Pacific—Marcia Stenson
2006	Scarecrow Army—Leon Davidson
2005	Welcome to the South Seas—Gregory O'Brien

- 兒童圖文書獎

* 2009 榮譽獎：Piggity-Wiggity Jiggity Jig—Diana Neild & Philip Webb

2009	Roadworks—Sally Sutton & Brian Lovelock
2008	Tahi— One Lucky Kiwi— Melanie Drewery, Ali Teo & John O'Reilly
2007	Kiss! Kiss! Yuck! Yuck! —Kyle Mewburn, Ali Teo & John O'Reilly
2006	A Booming in the Night —Ben Brown & Helen Taylor
2005	Clubs: A Lolly Leopold Story —Kate De Goldi, illustrated by Jacqui Colley

- 最佳新秀書獎

2009	Violence 101—Denis Wright
2008	Out of the Egg—Tina Matthews（also the 3rd winner of 2008 NZ Post Picture Book）
2007	The Three Fishing Brothers Bruff —Ben Galbraith
2006	The Unknown Zone — Phil Smith
2005	Cross Tides—Lorraine Orman

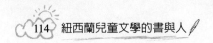

Writing for Children

in New Zealand

Joan Rosier-Jones

Contents

Writing for Children in New Zealand

Writing for children is alive and very well in New Zealand. It has not always been so. New Zealand is a young country. European habitation only began about 1840. Before that the Maori had been here for six hundred years or so. Their literary tradition was an oral one. Although there were no written stories, myths about the land and its people were handed down from generation to generation.

When the European settlers first arrived they were too intent on making a life in the new land to have time to write. Conditions were harsh for these pioneers. They had to carve arable land out of the bush, grow their own food and build homes with their bare hands. When there was time to write most authors wrote either poetry or for adults, imitating the tradition in the mother country, England. That is not to say there was nobody writing for children, but their work did not reach a wide public.

Once past the pioneering era, a lot of early writing for children was found in the School Journals, a series of magazines aimed at all levels of reading from the ages of six to twelve or thirteen. Many children's writers started their careers writing stories for the journals.

One of the best-loved novels for children is Elsie Locke's *The Runaway Settlers,* and that was not published until 1965. Since its publication this book has been in print continuously, longer than any other New Zealand children's book. This novel is based on the true story of a woman who ran away with her children from a violent husband in Sydney, Australia and began a new life as a pioneer in New Zealand. Her adventures included driving a herd of cattle over the Southern Alps in the South Island.

By the latter part of the 20th Century, children's writing had become so abundant and popular that annual book awards were offered for the best children's writing in several categories. One winner was Ken Catran a veteran writer for film and television. His novel, *Voyage with Jason* told the Greek myth of Jason and the Argonauts and their quest for the Golden Fleece in modern-day language.

Currently the awards are sponsored by New Zealand Post. World-renown author, Margaret Mahy is a consistent winner. She writes books at all levels from picture books to young adult fiction. Her stories are all imaginative. One favourite is *A Lion in the Meadow* and her young adult novels often deal with the supernatural. In spite of the fanciful nature of her stories, Margaret Mahy says that most of her ideas come from things that happen to her. 'But of course,'she adds, 'they are changed a great deal by the time the story is finished. The ideas begin with real things but I invent all sorts of things to add to them.'

Lynley Dodd, author and illustrator of the *Hairy Maclary* books also has an international reputation. Hairy Maclary is a dog who gets into all kinds of mischief. He is much loved by children the world over.

Another children's writer who is known throughout the world is William Taylor. His book, *Agnes the Sheep,* a chapter book for young readers (7-10 years old), has won many awards, including one in Italy. Agnes is described as maaad, baaad and dangerous. The book is in the "Hippo Funny" series of Ashton Scholastic and it certainly lives up to that. It is a very funny book.

Author, Joy Cowley, has also forged an international reputation for herself. She began writing for children to help her son, Edward, who like her, was slow to learn reading skills. *The Silent One* illustrated by Sherryl Jordan won the 1982 inaugural Children's Book of the Year. This poetically written book became a feature film, released in 1985 and tells the story of a deaf boy on a Pacific Island who befriends a white turtle.

Joy Cowley writes books for children of all ages including the young adult market. Other writers in this category include best-selling author, Tessa Duder, Gaelyn Gordon, Kate de Goldi and Margaret Beames. Margaret Beames was a finalist in the New Zealand Post awards with her dramatic science fiction work, *Outlanders*, and Tessa Duder won the award for 2000 with *The Tiggie Thompson Show* about a girl who desperately wants to be an actor.

New Zealand children love to read and they love meeting the authors of the books they read. The New Zealand Book Council runs a programme that takes writers into schools. This provides children with the opportunity to meet and talk to their favourite authors.

Every year a Storylines Festival of New Zealand Children's Writers and Illustrators is held in New Zealand's largest city, Auckland. An important feature of the festival is Family Day, a celebration where families meet writers and illustrators in a carnival atmosphere. There are many activities for children to join in. They can make their own books, learn to do calligraphy or try their own stories or plays out on writers and illustrators.

From a slow start, writing and illustrating for children has become one of the most popular genres in New Zealand. There is so much going on in this world of children's literature and so many authors involved that I cannot cover much here, but we will look at the following 22 chapters about these exciting writers.

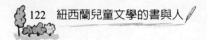

Margaret Mahy

New Zealand writer, Margaret Mahy, is one of the world's best-loved children's authors whose books have been translated into many different languages. She published her first book, *Lion in the Meadow*, in 1969 and it is still in print today. In the meantime she has published many, many more stories. Before she became a full-time writer in 1980, Margaret Mahy was the Children's Librarian at Canterbury Public Library in Christchurch.

Her highly imaginative writing ranges from poems and short stories to picture books for under fives and novels for young adults. Her short stories have been made into popular videos.

There is an element of the fantastic in much of her work. *The Witch in the Cherry Tree, Downhill Crocodile Whizz, The Girl With the Green Ear,* and *Elephant Milk, Hippopotamus Cheese* are typical titles. She often writes about the supernatural. Her young adult novels have titles like *Haunting, Dangerous Spaces* and *Dissolving Ghosts*. As Margaret Mahy herself says: 'I want the title to show clearly just what sort of book this is and who it is intended for. For *The Changeover* I gave the book a sub-title, *a supernatural romance*, so people would be warned.'

At the same time her stories are rooted in reality. The Mahy magic is to change the real into something completely unreal, and still make it believable. In *The Dragon of an Ordinary Family* the Belsaki family get a dragon for a pet. It is only a very small dragon to start with, but it grooooows. In fact it grows so big that the mayor insists they get rid of it. But how do you get rid of a pet, even if it is a dragon?

One picture book which is very real, however, is *One Summery Saturday Morning*. The setting is Mahy's beloved Governors Bay and the simple story of a mother goose who chases the dogs is charmingly told with repetition and rhyme.

> *The geese turn round and flap and hiss,*
> *Flap and hiss, flap and hiss.*
> *The dogs were not expecting this*
> *On a summery Saturday morning…*

Humour plays a large part in Margaret Mahy's work. In her poem, *Down the Back of the Chair*, the children's father loses his car keys and they look for them 'down the back of the chair'. And what do you find? Among other things 'A packet of pins and one of the twins…A crumb, a comb, a clown… a pirate with a treasure map…a dragon trying to take a nap.' And that's not all.

She also takes pleasure in using basic poetic techniques like alliteration, and the last verse of *Down the Back of the Chair* goes:

> *The chair, the chair, the challenging chair…*
> *The charming chair, the children's chair,*
> *The chopped and chipped but chosen chair…*

In a lesser writer's hands this might have been just too much repetition of the "ch" sound, but with Margaret Mahy it is pure delight. The repetition and rhythm tune us into the exuberance of the children who have been watching all these treasures appear from the back of their chair. You can see them dancing as they chant and sing the praises of their champion chair.

Margaret Mahy is also fond of word play. If there isn't a word to suit, she will make one up. The dog in the "Cousins Quartet" books is a "labradoodle", a cross between a labrador and a poodle. A mystery caller in the same series whispers, "Owangabangbootabotta" down the phone at one of the cousins. One of her books is entitled *Great Piratical Rumbustification.* In *17 Kings and 42 Elephants* you find words like "hippopotomums" "baboonsters" and "gorillicans".

It is obvious that Mahy loves the sound of words. Her stories are meant to be read out loud. She often tells people about an incident before deciding whether she will turn it into a story or not. 'I want to hear what the story *sounds* like,' she says.

New Zealand children are luckier than most because they sometimes get the chance to meet Margaret Mahy in the flesh, and Margaret Mahy in the flesh is something else. She wears funny costumes and a fluffy green wig, looking just like one of her own characters. Laughter is never far away.

Margaret Mahy has won many awards for her work, both in New Zealand and elsewhere.

In 1993 she was awarded The Order of New Zealand for her services to literature. She has two grown-up daughters and lives on Banks Peninsula with several cats and thousands on books in a house with a large garden.

Find out more about Margaret Mahy on http://library.christchurch. org.nz/Childrens/MargaretMahy

Joy Cowley

I was in the local library not long ago when a group of six-year-olds arrived for a visit. They were told to sit on the floor while the librarian read them a story. 'This story is by Joy Cowley,' the librarian said. A cry of delight rose up from the children. 'Joy Cowley. Joy Cowley. We *love* Joy Cowley.' I have never seen a group of six-year-olds sit as still as that little group did while the librarian read them *Captain Felonius*.

Captain Felonius is a bad tempered pirate. When something upset him he would swear so badly that the crew put their hands over their ears and the cat ran up the mast. His wife was worried. *'Now see here, my Dearie-o,' she said. 'Your swearing is really terrible. Why don't you give it up?'*

'I can't,' said the Captain. 'Sorry my little flower. But I just can't help it.' But the Captain's 'little flower' works out a plan. She gets him to write the words on a piece of paper instead of saying them, and in the end everyone except the crew are happy.

Like many writers Joy Cowley often uses the people and happenings around her for inspiration. The isolated farm at Fish Bay in the Marlborough Sounds at the top of the South Island of New Zealand where Joy Cowley lives has provided her with many stories.

When Joy Cowley left school her parents wanted her to become a pharmacist which she dutifully did. It was not until she was married and had children that she first thought of writing. She began writing children's stories for her son Edward who was a slow leaner.

From this her interest in using lively stories to capture the interest of young readers began. She spent the next twenty years or so writing early reading material. Many of these books are used in schools throughout the world.

The characters in these books are wonderful. They are real people we can all relate to, but at the same time they are larger-than-life. Among them are Dan the Flying Man, the Meanies, the Hungry Giant and Mrs Wishy-Washy. The idea for Mrs Wishy-Washy came about when Joy Cowley went winter fishing one day. When she got home, cold and wet, she soaked in a hot tub and as she splashed the water about, she thought, Wishy-washy, wishy-washy. What a good name.

Inspired by a long drought in the Marlborough region Joy Cowley wrote, *Singing Down the Rain*. In this story the town is suffering from the worst drought ever and the people are very depressed. Only a miracle can help them but they don't recognise the miracle when it turns up. It is the town's children who see that the mysterious woman who sings rain-songs is going to save them.

A firm favourite is *The Mouse Bride* illustrated by David Christiana. It retells an ancient Asian folk tale in which a very small mouse tries to find herself the biggest and strongest husband in the world so that she can have big, strong children. She asks the sun, a cloud, the wind and a tall wooden house to marry her. It is a story with a happy ending.

Some of her books have been so successful that they have developed into a series. *Agapanthus Hum* is one. If it's all right to call a child Rose, or Lily or Violet, then why not Agapanthus? It too is a flower. Agapanthus Hum is based on Joy Cowley's own daughter,

Judith, who wore glasses from the age of nine months. "Judith was a vigorous, athletic and very cheerful child," Joy Cowley explains. "I can't remember how many glasses were dropped, sat on, broken, lost. One pair was flushed down the toilet. Another pair went under the lawnmower. Judith was always optimistic, did her best to take care of her glasses, but when you rush at life with a song and a somersault, the best isn't quite good enough. Years later I decided to create Agapanthus Hum, a character modelled on my own sweet Judith."

Joy Cowley is a frequent visitor to New Zealand schools where she encourages children to write their own stories. In *The Day of the Wind* she tells the story of the children of Chapel Down School who were making wonderful stories about all sorts of things – giants, dinosaurs, a spacewoman, a twenty-metre* hot dog and more. Sadly the windows were open and the wind picked up the stories and away they flew.

> *The wind went haa-aa!*
> *The wind went hoo-hoo!*
> *It chuckled and cackled*
> *And chortled and blew.*
> *The wind whistled up*
> *The wind whistled down.*
> *It took the stories into the town…*

Luckily the children finally caught the stories, but not before the people of the town had read them and realised what gifted writers the children were. "The people in the shopping mall said to the children, 'Fantiddlytastic! This is the best day we've ever had! Write some more wonderful stories soon."

---

* metre = meter

Joy Cowley's work covers all aspects of writing. Here we have only looked at her picture books, but she also writes children's and adults' fiction and non-fiction. She has won many awards for her writing the latest being the Junior Fiction category of the New Zealand Post Awards for her junior novel, *Shadrach Girl*. Her contribution to New Zealand literature has also been recognized beyond the literary industry. In 1992 she was awarded the Order of the British Empire and the following year a Doctorate in Literature from Massey University. She is a Patron of the New Zealand Children's Book Foundation.

Find out more about Joy Cowley on: http://www.joycowley.com

William Taylor

William Taylor's work has been described as 'contemporary realism in rural and small-town settings.' In this it is unlike much of the more imaginative writing of many New Zealand children's authors. That is not to say the writing lacks invention. Far from it. William Taylor's stories are well plotted and are tales of humour and compassion. Noticeable aspects are his acute ear for dialogue and strong characterization.

William Taylor was born in Lower Hutt close to the capital city, Wellington, and began his working life in a bank before going to Teachers' Training College. He taught in London and schools around New Zealand before settling in Raurimu, Mount Ruapehu. Here he not only became principal of the local primary school, but was also mayor of Ohakune for seven years.

Before writing for children William Taylor wrote four adult novels. He now regards those as the apprenticeship for his 'real' work – writing for children. He finds children the most rewarding audience. He says: 'I think I am able to reflect on what it is like to be young and growing up in New Zealand society today and have an ability to capture the hopes and fears, the joys and sadnesses and the uncertainties that children face in this day and age.' He is well prepared for the task having been a teacher for over twenty years. Other experiences are also useful. 'I have been young myself (a long time ago),' he explains. 'I have reared children of my own. I was a solo parent for very many years, and getting a couple of sons through adolescence has given me enough ammunition for a thousand novels!'

He is one of New Zealand's most prolific authors, but did not start writing fulltime until he was almost fifty. Indeed there are so many books it would not be productive to try and discuss too many of them here, so we will only cover a few of my favourites from the 8-11 rage here.

One of the most successful books is *Agnes the Sheep*. In 1991 this won William Taylor the most prestigious prize in New Zealand children's literature, the Esther Glen Award. It also won the Premio Andersen prize in Italy, `1998. Like many of Taylor's books it has been translated into many languages.

Agnes the sheep is *Maaaad...baaaad and dangerous to know.* She is bequeathed to two children, Joe and Belinda, by old Mrs Carpenter just before she dies. Agnes is a dirty, smelly sheep that butts anyone who is silly enough to get in her way. So Belinda and Joe have a job on their hands taking care of her. This book is published in the 'Hippo Funny' series of Ashton Scholastic and a funnier book is hard to find, as the two children try to hide Agnes from Mrs Carpenter's greedy relations who want to see her dead and made into mutton chops.

In *Agnes the Sheep* William Taylor covers some weighty subjects like honesty and death, but he never preaches. His touch is light, a take-it-or-leave-it attitude towards the 'message'.

Knitwits is both serious and funny too, but in a different way. Charlie Kenny, the first-person narrator of the book begins like this:

> *Our cat croaked this morning*
> *I got tossed off our hockey team this afternoon.*

Then to top things off, Mum told me she was going to have a
baby.
It was one of those days.

It is the baby who occupies Charlie throughout the book and he gets himself into a bet with his neighbour, Alice Pepper because of it. The bet? To knit the baby a sweater. *Does Charlie know how to knit? No! Will he die of embarrassment if anyone catches him? Yes!* Will the baby die of embarrassment when it has to wear Charlie's Technicolor 'oblongs' which is what he calls the front, back and two sleeves of the sweater? Probably.

Knitwits is about not caring what others think of you. At the end of the book you are left wondering how Charlie will get on with the new arrival. The sequel is called *Numbskulls* and it begins:

The way some people tell it, babies do nothing more than eat
and sleep. These people can only be deaf, blind and have no
noses! ...Some people reckon babies are just like little rose
buds. Whew! Let me tell you, the smells that come from our
baby are nothing like the smells you get from even a half-nice
rosebud.

Charlie is not very clever and is worried that he will not be a good enough brother for the new baby. Alice Pepper lures him into her back shed where sits her amazing learning machine. Alice promises Charlie that the machine will make him a smart speller. Charlie climbs aboard with some surprising results.

Moralising is too strong a word for what William Taylor does, but in *Numbskulls* the lightly given message is – if you really put your mind to something you can do it, but it's okay to just be

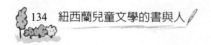

yourself. There are similar carefully concealed messages in all William Taylor's books. But above all they are some of the funniest books around.

William Taylor has been National President of the New Zealand Society of Authors (note). His excellence as a writer has been recognised in many awards, fellowships and grants. For a list of these and some of his other works go to: http://www.bookcouncil. org.nz/writers/taylorwilliam.html

Note: In September 2001 the Oceanian Chinese Writers' Association (OCWA) and the New Zealand Society of Authors (NZSA) established a joint fellowship. As the National President of NZSA, William Taylor signed the agreement between these two sister organisations; and two years later in March 2003 he attended a Chinese Writers' Conference in Taipei where he gave a speech on behalf of NZSA.

Tessa Duder

Tessa Duder's advice to aspiring authors is to be curious about the world around them and to do lots of interesting things in order to be an interesting person. 'Then later,' she explains, 'you will have something to say.' This New Zealand author has certainly taken her own advice. When she was 18 she was a silver medalist in the swimming at the 1958 Empire Games (later called the Commonwealth Games). She is widely travelled having lived in London, Pakistan and Malaysia; she is an experienced sailor and an accomplished actor. All this experience has served her well as a writer.

Tessa Duder's first novel, *Night Race toKawau,* (1982) tells the story of how one family copes when the father, the only experienced sailor on board, is knocked unconscious at the beginning of a yacht race. Here are the elements that distinguish her later work – powerful female characters and a strong, dramatic plot.

Tessa Duder says: 'There is a huge responsibility but no great mystery in being a writer for children. Yes, it is the only genre that is not written by someone from the intended readership. Successful children's writers must first be fine writers. They have however worked hard to maintain both a 'hot line' back to their childhood and direct contact with children. From these come the truthfulness and integrity which are the hallmarks of good writing for children.'

Duder is perhaps best known internationally for a quartet of young adult novels based on a young athlete, Alex. These award-winning books have been published in USA, Britain and Australia as well as being translated into several different languages.

Alex, like Duder herself, is a swimmer. In the first book she is training to qualify for the Commonwealth Games. As well she is trying to keep up with her studies, the hockey team and life in general. Duder knows herself only too well the demands swimming at the highest level can place on a young person. Alex is a positive role model and young people around the world love the four books in the series. *Alex* was made into a successful feature film and as a follow-up Duder wrote a book about the making of the movie to give young people an insight into the process involved in translating a book to the screen.

Her later works are also based on an abiding interest – the theatre and acting. *The Tiggie Thompson Show* is about a girl, Antigone Thompson, who struggles with her sense of self, and through the drama club at school becomes involved in acting for television. The back cover invites the reader to 'Join Tiggie for the most astonishing year of her life…' and it is quite a journey. This novel won the 2000 New Zealand Post Children's Book Award. The sequel is *Tiggie Thompson All At sea*. Tiggie has won the role of Eliza in a 19th century drama and while she researches the period to help her with the role she becomes increasingly caught up in the character. There are further complications when she hears from a half-brother in Australia.

Tessa Duder says she writes for children because: 'I regard it as the greatest privilege – that my imperfect story should be put in front of young minds that are still capable of generosity, of accepting new ideas, of being entertained and amused and informed. Similarly if my story does not engage them, or it is inappropriate to their age, they will let me know soon enough.'

Over the years she has developed close working liaisons and friendships with many New Zealand writers, particularly those writing for children. The result of one such friendship was the book she co-wrote with William Taylor. In *Hot Mail* they established two characters – 14-year-old Jess who is sailing the Pacific on a yacht with her mother and step-father, and Dan 'dantheman' who lives in small town New Zealand. Jess and Dan correspond by e-mail. They get off to a shaky start. '*You know what they say about computers,*' Jess e-mails Dan under the heading 'Garbage'. '*Garbage in (which is you) and garbage out (which is your e-mails). I don't think you're 22, I don't even think you're nine. I think you're about eleven with a reading age of seven and braindead basically.*' In spite of this their relationship develops but they have no idea how strong it will become and how important it is to Jess's survival as the yacht sails into the hurricane season.

Tessa Duder has also edited several anthologies aimed at the young adult reader, among them *Falling in Love, Nearly seventeen* and *Personal Best,* stories about sporting achievement by some of Australia's and New Zealand's best authors for young adults.

She has won awards and literary bursaries for her writing. She is active in writers' politics and was the President of the New Zealand Society of Authors 1996-1998. She has played a large part in the establishment of the New Zealand Children's Book Foundation. She was awarded the OBE (Order of the British Empire) in 1994 for her services to New Zealand literature and the Children's Book Foundation's recognition of achievement, the Margaret Mahy Medal in 1996.

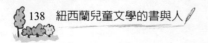

Find out more about Tessa Duder on: http://www.bookcouncil.
org.nz/writers/duder.html

Lynley Dodd

Lynley Dodd had written and illustrated several children's books before she became a world-renown author. She won the 1978 Choysa Children's Writers Bursary and the 1981 New Zealand Book Award for her illustrations in Clarice England's *Druscilla*. But that was nothing compared with what was to come.

In 1983 *Hairy Maclary from Donaldson's Dairy* made his first appearance. Written and illustrated by Lynley Dodd it is the story of a mischievous dog. The author has a very good eye for animal behaviour and a keen ear for rhyme. Her illustrations are full of witty detail. The judges of the Children's Picture Book of the Year Award recognised this. They awarded her the main prize. She was to win this prize again and again. She has written over 20 picture books and received 20 awards for her work in children's literature. Almost every child in New Zealand knows Hairy Maclary, his friends and foes, but these books and many others have also been published worldwide.

So what is all the fuss about? It is difficult to discuss Lynley Dodd's work in words because the illustrations provide such a strong sub-text and so much humour. Words alone will not do justice to the work, but I will try to give you some idea of Lynley Dodd's charm. One of my favourite Hairy Maclary books is *Hairy Maclary's Show Business*. The Cat Club is having its annual show and Hair Maclary has been tied up to a tree in the street outside. He is not happy...*He struggled and squirmed, he unravelled the knot and dragging his lead, he was off at the trot.* As you can imagine he upsets the cats waiting in their cages for their turn to be shown. The cats' owners try to catch him, but Hairy Maclary is *slippery slick.* He leads them on a chase until Miss Plum captures him. She does not recognise Hairy Maclary for what he is and guess who *won the prize for the SCRUFFIEST CAT?*

But Hair Maclary from Donaldson's Dairy is not the only animal in Lynley Dodd's menagerie. There is the daschund dog, Schnitzel von Krumm with a very low tum; the cat Slinky Malinki and the parrot, Stickybeak Syd. Another cat, this one to be feared, is Scarface Claw, the toughest tomcat in town. The animals sometimes star in their own stories, but often appear together. In *Hairy Maclary Scattercat* Hairy Maclary chases the neighbourhood cats all over the place. Slinky Malinki is one of these frightened cats. *Slinky Malinki was down in the reeds. BUT ALONG CAME HAIRY MACLARY...and hustled him into a drum full of weeds.* But wait. Hair Maclary takes on one cat too many – Scarface Claw! Scarface chases poor Hairy all the way home. As you can imagine Scarface is very pleased with himself.

In *Slinky Malinki, Open the Door* Slinky and Stickybeak Syd get up to mischief in the empty house. They open the doors and create a mess in all the rooms. The last door they open is the front door. Can you guess who is waiting to get in? Not only Hairy Maclary, but five of his doggy friends. The hair on Slinky Malinki's back stands on end and Stickybeak Syd flies away. They won't open that door again in a hurry.

When she was a little girl Lynley Dodd lived in the Kaingaroa Forest settlement a long way from the nearest town. Her school consisted of one room. There were only a few children and there was no library. 'I learned to rely on my own resources and imagination. Looking back, I don't ever remember having been bored. When I wasn't involved in endless flights of imagination outdoors with any available children, I was reading avidly or drawing.' The absence of a library was not a problem because the family had books sent to them from the National Library. Lynley Dodd remembers: '…the delicious feeling of anticipation when the box was opened and the delights therein revealed.'

Before becoming a fulltime writer, Lynley Dodd taught art at Queen Margaret College in Wellington. Now she lives with her husband and pet cat Pipi. Her house is in the country, providing the peace and quiet for her to work. Here she sits at a large desk in a workroom with a beautiful view of the countryside. She has two grown-up children. Lynley Dodd was made a Distinguished Companion of the New Zealand Order of Merit – a very high honour indeed.

For a comprehensive list of Lynley Dodd's work go to: http://www.bookcouncil.org.nz/writers/doddlynley.html

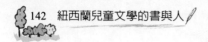

Margaret Beames

Like many writers for children, Margaret Beames was an avid reader as a child. 'I was never happier than when I was lost in a book. It seemed a natural progression to write my own stories, although it was not until after I emigrated to New Zealand in my late thirties that I began to write with a view to publication.'

Margaret Beames was born in Oxford, England and again, like many writers for children began her working life as a teacher. Since her first book, *The Greenstone Summer* published in 1977, she has published thirty books. They range from picture books to stories for young adults. *Oliver in the Garden*, illustrated by Sue Hitchcock won the New Zealand Post Picture Book and Children's Choice categories in 2001. *Outlanders* was shortlisted for the Senior Fiction category in the same awards.

She says: 'Looking back I can see how my reading as a child opened up to me a whole world of people and cultures far removed from the small town where I grew up. It also fed my imagination and helped me understand the world around me. Now, when I write for children, I hope I am doing as much for them.'

She certainly is. Here we will look at just two of her books for older readers *Archway Arrow* (1996) and *Outlanders* (2000), both favourites of mine. I bought *Outlanders* for my nephew's tenth birthday. He became instantly unsociable. While we enjoyed his birthday party, he could not take drag himself away from the story.

'A rich imagination makes for a fuller life,' Margaret Beames told me. 'Above all, though, books should be a pleasure. I see myself first and foremost as a story teller.'

Outlanders fulfills all these requirements. It is richly imaginative, a great story and a pleasure to read. A futuristic book it opens with the "Great Disaster", the landing of an enormous asteroid on earth when ...*Temperatures plummeted. The Global winter had begun.* We see the last people arrive at the Dome which will allow humans to survive in artificial surroundings.

> *...at the entrance she stopped abruptly. Up close the fabric of the dome was silver with a texture like sharkskin. It soared massively into the sky...There were no windows in it. She turned for one last look at the outside world, at the ring of the distant hills.*
>
> *'What's the matter?' he said, suddenly afraid that after all she might yet back away...*
>
> *'It's okay. I was just thinking – we won't see another sunset. Not a real one.'*
>
> *...Behind them the doors slid shut with a whisper like silk.*

The couple is the last allowed into the Dome. The people left outside became the Outlanders of the title. They were reputed to have become grotesque monsters, every child's bogeyman. The story then shifts ahead 200 years to the narrative of a talented art student, Rhiane a'Dare. She has painted a picture so shocking that it cannot be displayed. Now there are rumours that Rhiane has been 'outside' and is causing a deadly epidemic for those living in the Dome.

'There is no doubt,' Margaret says, 'that the speed with which we live life today, and the influence of television in particular, have affected the way I now approach my work. I must catch the reader's attention on the first page and the plot must move forward at a brisk pace, but there's still a time and place for lyrical writing.'

Here is Rhiane's lyrical reaction to 'outside': *Tree trunks are not just brown or grey. They are all shades between with splodges of green, orange, yellow...I crushed a handful of low-hanging leaves against my face. They smelt spicy and clean.*

Archway Arrow is for slightly younger readers, 9-12. Stefan and Colin have a problem. They want to enter the raft race and win a thousand dollars for Archway School. But they have little money and next to no time. They find their crew, Trish, Annie, Scott and Jamie, but Jamie can't swim and his mother won't let him near the water. What is more, their rivals, the Rainford Rats get up to some dirty tricks to try and put them out of the race.

Scott was examining the raft for damage. 'Look at this,' he said. 'Someone's been trying to cut the lashing.' He pointed out the frayed edges... 'Look you can see where the knife scratched the metal.'...'And hey, look at this,' Trish went on. 'The mooring rope's been cut.'

On race day one of the Rainford Rats falls off their raft and the Archway team pick him up. This slows them down and they cross the line in second place. But there is a surprising twist as Mr Hubert, who donated the thousand dollars, hands out the prize.

Margaret is part of the Writers in Schools scheme organised by the New Zealand Book Council and is much loved by the children she talks to. She is a modern writer and her first e-book *Josef's Bear* can be found on www.ebooksonthe.net She lives with her husband, their dog and hens in a country home near Feilding in the North Island. She has two children and six grandchildren.

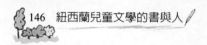

Find out more about Margaret Beames on: http://www.bookcouncil. org.nz/writers/beamesmargaret.html

Sheryll Jordan

The story of Sheryll Jordan's life as an author would warm the heart of many a would-be writer. She had written and illustrated twenty-seven picture books and twelve novels over seven years. Only three of the children's books were published and not one of the novels. The turning point came in 1991 when her thirteenth novel, *Rocco*, (entitled *A Time of Darkness* for the American market) was published.

But even after publication life did not get easier. Since 1990 Sheryll Jordan has suffered from Occupational Overuse Syndrome. As an artist this was disastrous. Not only did she have to give up drawing, but also her other hobbies such as weaving, yachting, motorbike riding and screen printing. It was only with great difficulty that she continued writing. She has tried a voice-activated programme for her computer with little success.

In spite of that she has had many titles published and has also illustrated some of Joy Cowley's work. She is a full-time writer who also speaks to schools, seminars and conferences around the world on writing for children.

Sheryll Jordan has won many awards both in New Zealand and overseas. *Winter of Fire* has consistently been in Whitcoulls, New Zealand-wide bookstores Top 100 Books and was voted 'Young Adults' Choice' in USA, 1995. In 2001 she won seven awards in New Zealand, Germany and USA. One of those was the New

Zealand Children's Literature Foundation Margaret Mahy Medal and Lecture Award for making a significant contribution to children's literatre, publishing and literacy. One notable award was for *The Raging Quiet* which won the prestigious Literaturhaus prize in Vienna for the Best Book for Young People. Her books are published in USA, England and have been translated into many languages.

Of her work Sheryll Jordan says: 'All my young adult novels have been gifts. I don't think them up. They hit me over the head when I least expect them; overwhelm me with impressions, sights and sounds of their new worlds; enchant me with their characters; and dare me to write them.'

Most stories are set during the medieval period and that life is evoked clearly and believably, often in small, almost loving detail.

Catherine was wrapping some bread and cheese in a small cloth. She put the food and a small leather bottle of water into a drawstring bag and tied it to Minstrel's belt. ('Sign of the Lion', 1995.)

Sheryll Jordan goes on to explain: 'Some books are inspired by a character who suddenly, dramatically comes into my vision and my heart.'

Among my favourite characters is Denzil from the *Wednesday Wizard* series for ten to twelve-year-olds. The year is 1291 and Denzil is an apprentice wizard who lives in a medieval village. Old Mother Wyse warns him to beware of Spy Wednesday, the large town and the dragon. Denzil thinks the warning is intended for his master, Wizard Valvasor. He tries to pass on the warning by using one of Valvasor's spells. Sadly the spell goes wrong – very wrong – and Denzil arrives seven centuries into the future, landing in the backyard of the MacAllister family. The story follows the mixed fortunes of Denzil and Samantha (Sam) MacAllister as Denzil tries to convince the family that he really is a medieval wizard, and as he tries to find his way back to his own time to warn Valvassor. In the third book in this series Denzil meets Wimpy, a dancing bear. He is horrified when he learns how the bear is made to move – by making it dance on a hot plate. There is nothing for it, but to rescue the bear and take him to Sam and her family. Of course, it's not that easy time-travelling with a bear.

Another favourite is Elsha, heroine of *Winter of Fire*. She is a child of the Quelled – an outcast people who have to mine coal for the ruling class, the Chosen. Elsha is a rebel with a vision. On her sixteenth birthday she has a dream of a better world for all the Quelled. She sets about finding it, in spite of the fact that she might die because of her actions. 'She is the light in a world of darkness,' the cover proclaims. She was the light in her author's darkness also. *Winter of Fire* was written one line at a time at first when Sheryll Jordan was suffering badly from Occupational Overuse Syndrome. At the beginning of the book Sheryll Jordan pays tribute to Elsha. 'It was because of her that I refused to accept that my writing days were over...We were warriors together in our battles against the impossible...'

Another warrior of a different kind, but still of the same era is Minstrel in *Sign of the Lion*. The night she is born her father pledges her in return for his wife's life. When she is twelve the mysterious woman comes to the village to claim her. Minstrel has her guardian angel, Elmo, to keep an eye on her, but even so it is no easy task resisting the cruel Griselda. But Minstrel is destined for greatness if she can only find her way out of the dark forest and out of Griselda's evil clutches.

Sheryll Jordan lives in Tauranga with her husband, Lee and cat Jethro. She has one grown-up daughter.

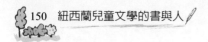

　　Find out more about Sheryll Jordan on: http://www.bookcouncil. org.nz/writers/jordansherryl.html

David Hill

David Hill was born in 1940. He studied at Victoria University in Wellington receiving a Master of Arts with Honours in 1964. He was a secondary teacher for 14 years, and this obviously helped his extensive understanding of what interests adolescent boys. He started writing, though, he says in order to write about his own children when they were little.

David Hill became a fulltime writer in 1978. He is a journalist, reviewer and playwright as well as a children's author. His first teenage novel *See Ya Simon* was published in 1992 and it has been winning awards ever since. Among the awards are the Times Educational Supplement (UK) Award for Special Needs in 1994 and the Gaelyn Gordon Best-Loved New Zealand Book.

See Ya Simon is about a 14-year-old boy who is dying of muscular dystrophy. It is written with a down-to-earth attitude and such humour that it is never overly emotional.

David Hill's next three novels look at the problems of the lonely teenage outsider. The stories are set against backgrounds of a variety of interests. *Kick Back*, is about Tae Kwon Do, a tramping trip goes badly wrong in *Take It Easy*, and *The Winning Touch* is about a rugby team. Those three books were all published in 1995. *Give It Hoops*, 1988, tells the story of the Mt Andrews' basketball team The books are thoroughly researched. Here is the description of a basketball game in *Give It Hoops*:

Marc shot up-court on one of his breaks. Again Hamish was blocked, but Brooke seized his bounce pass and scored. Back came Merrilands, and scored also. A series of struggling, battling intercepts and blockings on both sides of the court...

Not all the novels are about sport. *Curtain Up,* is about a group involved in a stage production. The cover of *Fat Four-Eyed and Useless,* 1997, proclaims:

Makes me sick, the way everyone goes on about sport, sport, SPORT! I'm useless at sport. In fact, I'm fat, four-eyed and useless...

This book, for slightly younger children, is about Ben who finds himself through writing. It is illustrated with funny line drawings and told in the form of a diary. Like all the other stories this has its share of humour.

I shared Mum's carrot cake with everyone. Mel had two pieces. 'I'm a light eater,' she said. 'I eat as soon as it's light.'

In *Impact* Fraser belongs to an astronomy club. He loves watching the night sky through the six-inch telescope, but one night he sees more than he bargained for. A meteor flashes across the sky and crashes nearby. There is a race to find it. And a struggle to keep it.

Fraser is a very real person. When the story opens he is an unpopular 'geek'. Pupils from his school go on a trip to the observatory where Fraser helps out.

'That's the geek from last night,' Fraser heard a voice mutter as he came out of the Science Block next morning.

He didn't look. Five seconds later he thought of the perfect answer. 'Pleased to meet you,' he should have told the kid. 'I hear you're a geek every night.' Typical – always five seconds too late.

By the end of the book Fraser is something of a hero and he has a girlfriend, Courtenay with the 'sun-coloured' hair and clear blue eyes. A sub-plot deals with Fraser's older sister who has left school to go off with her boyfriend and his band. Now she is home again, pregnant. A hallmark of David Hill's writing is that he is not afraid to look at real-life issues such as teenage pregnancy. A sub-plot in *Fat, Four-eyed and Useless* is about Ben's father losing his job. In *Time Out* Kit goes running to escape the pain of his parents' break-up and his mother's drinking problem.

The boyfriend/girlfriend relationship is a theme common to most of the stories. *Time Out*'s Kit is another lonely boy who finds his soul-mate in green-eyed Erica. While out running Kit is mysteriously swallowed up by a 'black cloud-mouth' and so arises the possibility of a parallel universe:

There may be billions of parallel universes. Every time you choose a different jacket in a different world. Every one of these universes will be partly the same and partly different.

David Hill enjoys writing. 'It's the feeling that you've made something,' he says. 'Lots of other people will make much better things than you, but no one will ever make the same. What you've done is unique and that's marvellous.'

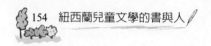

David lives in New Plymouth in the North Island with his wife, Beth. His hobbies are tramping, reading and cheering for the All Blacks. His books have been translated into Estonian, French and Chinese.

Find out more about David Hill on http://www.bookcouncil. org.nz/writers/hilldavid.html

Gavin Bishop

Gavin Bishop was born in Invercargill at the bottom of the South Island of New Zealand in 1946. His mother's family was of Maori descent, and he looks at Maori culture in several of his books. He graduated in 1967 from Canterbury University's School of Fine Arts with honours in painting. For 30 years he taught art in Christchurch secondary schools.

Like so many other writers Gavin Bishop was an avid reader as a child. He says : 'I joined the public library and discovered the joys of a free library system. *The Hobbit* introduced itself to me through an extract in a school journal when I was nine. I have read it several times since then and still find it a source of inspiration.'

Bishop is widely travelled and has visited many countries throughout the world, including China. In 1992 he was invited to Beijing and Shanghai by UNESCO to lecture and run workshops on Children's Literature.

Unlike many New Zealand writers, Gavin Bishop very quickly established his reputation as a writer and illustrator. The first book he wrote and illustrated was published immediately and several books quickly followed. He is very much a visual storyteller, using illustration to add detail to the text.

He has won so many awards we haven't the room here to mention them all. Among them are New Zealand Post Children's Book Awards Book of the year in 1999 for *The House That Jack*

Built, (Scholastic, 1999). This is based on an old nursery rhyme which Bishop has satirised. Jack symbolises the colonising European who ignores the traditions of the Maori people as he builds not only his house, but a whole town. Papatuanuku, the earth mother, watches in despair.

Several other books explore the theme of the mythical mother goddess. *Hinepau* (Scholastic, 1993) won New Zealand Picture Book of the Year in 1993. It is the story of a young Maori woman who uses her weaving to save her tribe from the aftermath of a volcanic eruption. The illustrations are dark and present a sense of foreboding, until the end when Hinepau creates a glorious sunset. The next day dawns brightly and life begins again.

Another book with sombre and mystical illustrations is *The Horror of Hickory Bay*, (Oxford University Press, 1984). A young girl, India Brown and her 'Uncle Athol' who looks suspiciously like a puppet, are camping with India Brown's parents. Although they have just had Christmas dinner – a barbecue on the beach which is quite proper in New Zealand where Christmas comes in the middle of a hot summer – India Brown says she is still hungry.

'HUNGRY?' a thunderous voice boomed.

It's the Horror of Hickory Bay who attempts to eat everything in sight – fish, trees, cars, caravans. There are few words:

'GLUMP!' goes the monster on one page.
'SLURP! GULP!' he shouts on another.

The illustrations carry much of the story. They are often humorous as on the last page when India Brown and Uncle Athol, with the help of the Smudge the dog, have saved the day. Mum offers India Brown a sausage. India Brown isn't hungry any more, but Smudge is. You have to look carefully, but there he is in the corner of the illustration, his tongue hanging out hungrily.

But not all Gavin Bishop's stories are about the violent forces of nature. Gavin Bishop says: '...to survive financially, a children's writer in a country as small as New Zealand, needs to publish globally...'

To accomplish this he has had to study the various markets. The American market he claims requires an 'air of innocence and sweetness.'

One of my favourite Gavin Bishop characters which fits this bill is Little Rabbit who not only features in books, but has also appeared on greeting cards and posters. *Little Rabbit and the Sea*, is a simply told story of longing and the realisation of a dream. Little Rabbit wants to see the sea. ...*every night he dreamed of being a sailor.* The first illustration shows Little Rabbit in bed, his arm tucked lovingly around a sailing boat. There is a lighthouse on the bedside table, wallpaper decorated with boats, gulls and waves. Even the bed cover has a wavy look. It looks like Little Rabbit is obsessed with the idea of the sea. He asks everyone he knows what the sea is like and finally a sea gull takes him to see for himself. The sea was everything Little Rabbit had expected.

Animals also feature in *Stay Awake Bear*, (Orchard Books, New York, 2000), a finalist in the Book Awards for 2001. As you probably know, bears hibernate in winter, but Old Bear and Brown Bear decide that '*sleeping is a waste of time*'. So when the other bears get ready for winter Old Bear and Brown Bear stay awake and plan their summer holiday.

And when the days lengthened and the snow melted, they packed their bags and set off. But by the time they reached the station, they were both yawning.

And they sleep all through their summer holiday. However when winter comes round again they are wide awake. This is a wonderful story, particularly for children who don't want to go to bed.

Gavin Bishop has written and designed two ballets for the Royal New Zealand Ballet Company. He now lives in Christchurch with his wife, Vivienne. He has a grown-up family and no pets since the local cats ate the last of their goldfish.

Find out more about Gavin Bishop on http://www.gavinbishop.com

Ken Catran

Ken Catran began his writing life 28 years ago as a scriptwriter for television. During this time he twice received the Best Script Award. Among his many scripts were dramas for children and finally he decided to break away and concentrate on writing books for children.

He is a versatile writer whose subject matter ranges across time and space, from small town New Zealand to science fiction, from the two World Wars to ancient myth.

Voyage With Jason (Lothian 2001) is the re-telling of the myth Jason and the Argonauts. So successfully did Catran accomplish this tale of the search for the Golden Fleece that he won the New Zealand Post's Senior Fiction category and Book of the Year for 2001. Another myth retold is *Golden Prince*, (Lothian, 2002) the story of Pyrrhus, who leads the troops at the siege of Troy.

Fries (Lothian Books, 2002) is a book much closer to home for Ken Catran. In this contemporary novel, the factory that makes French fries is about to close. In the small town where Catran lives there is a similar factory. *Fries* is a what-if story. What if the 'fries' factory closed? According to Catran, gravestones will fly and the Fries Phantom will haunt the town. But things are not as they seem. In unfolding the mystery of the Fries Phantom 14-year-old Paul Knox, uncovers a long-forgotten crime as well as saving the town.

Ken Catran writes great characters. Paul Knox is one such. Another is, Mike Connors in *Talking To Blue* (Lothian Books, 2000 and shortlisted for New Zealand Post Book Awards) and its sequel *Blue Murder*. Sharing the limelight with Mike is his friend, Sheril Anderson ...*tall, brown-haired and very good to look at. Talking to Blue* starts chillingly with *It all began on the Monday with another murder.* Blue talks to Mike by phone between stalking and killing the townsfolk. He is 'evil with no face'. On a lighter side Sheril and Mike have an interesting relationship. When Mike scores at rugby, Sheril says:

> *'We just have to prove ourselves, don't we Mike Connors? Just the hottest thing there is, eh?'*
> *...* *'Just about the hottest thing there is, honey.'* She hates being called 'honey'. *'Are you on offer?'*
> *'I might be.'* She comes closer, prods one finger a little hard under my chin. *'My present boyfriend's a really up-himself jerk.'*
> *'He must have something going for him,' I say, still grinning because I'm the up-himself jerk.'*

Among the science fiction books are the "Deepwater Trilogy" and "The Solar Colonies" series which have sold approximately 50,000 copies throughout the world.

'I find the term 'science fiction' to be a misnomer,' Ken Catran explains, 'because much of this kind of writing has become 'science fact' and for the novels I am writing now, I prefer the term 'futuristic fiction'. I like to pitch them perhaps 20 years ahead of the present, even less, so that the readers have a contemporary picture, enhanced only by the growth of hi-tech.'

Space Wolf (Harper Collins, 1994) is one of the science fiction stories. One wonders if the six-legged creature that crash-lands in the bush will ever really appear on earth. Two kids, Tendo and Monk find this space wolf, as Monk explains:

> *Then I saw a humped outline and jointed stalk-legs; one of them showed in the sun, ending in a round metal button. The thing red-flashed at us again and pulled its legs back into the shadow. We heard a hissing, spluttering noise that sounded angry and dangerous...*

They call it Urk because that is the sound it makes.

Both boys have lost a parent and they become convinced that the new arrival will be able to help them sort out their lives. Then comes decision time. As Monk's mother, who is a vet, puts it, Urk is like a dog, trained by two different masters. Is their new six-legged friend the most wonderful thinking machine ever? Or is it the deadliest man-made wolf-monster out of space.

Several books deal with war themes, using a historical perspective in a modern setting. One such is *Focus and the Death-Ride* (Harper Collins, 1994). Its opening passage gives the impression of a science-fiction story:

It was black outside and The Owl was hunting us. This owl was more than just a night-flying bird, it was a monster spitting death...

In one sense it is science fiction, but in another it takes us back in time, rather than forward. It is a wonderfully plotted story which makes imaginative use of history as Mad Perce McAllister tells Bryce and his girlfriend, Focus, his war stories.

In 1996 Ken Catran was the writer-in-residence at Dunedin College of Education. He still dabbles in writing for the screen but now he is adapting his own novels for film and television.

Ken Catran lives in Waimate, a small town in South Canterbury in the South Island with his wife. He likes walking and reading – especially reference books which provide him with a wide range of inspirational topics such as dinosaurs, ancient civilisations and outer space.

Find out more about Ken Catran on http://www.bookcouncil. org.nz/writers/catranken.html

Pamela Allen

Pamela Allen is an award-winning author and illustrator. She has published thirty picture books in twenty-two years. Children around the world enjoy her books. The original English has been translations into French, Swedish and Japanese.

Meg Sorensen of *Australian Book Review* said: 'With a Pamela Allen picture book we are mesmerised from the first illustration – it is a deceptively simple yet completely enchanted world.'

One such book is *Fancy That*. This is the story of a little red hen hatching her chicks. Pamela Allen says: 'This is a book to share with the very young. Here words merge with noises and the sounds of the fowl-yard can be heard for miles around.'

In *Fancy That* the hen goes TOOK, TOOK, TOOK. Her chicks go cheep, cheep, cheep and the rooster goes, COCK-A-DOODLE-DOO.

'I write for children who cannot read,' says Pamela Allen. 'This means that someone must read my books aloud. Now there is a voice. A voice that can whisper, shout, laugh or squeal. A voice that can grunt, neigh or quack.'

Animals feature frequently in Pamela Allen's work. *My Cat Maisie* (Hodder & Stoughton, 1990) won the New Zealand AIM Children's Picture Book of the Year Award in 1991. A stray cat comes to Andrew's house and he wants it to stay. He shows the cat all the games he can play:

> 'Let's play wild Indians and you can be the horse,' said
> Andrew.
> 'Let's be helicopters and whizz round and round...'

The illustrations show the poor cat looking very unhappy at the rough games Andrew wants to play. The cat, understandably, runs away. Then Andrew gets some of his own medicine when the dog next-door tries to play rough with him. The story does have a happy ending, though. That night the cat comes to Andrew's bedroom window. He lets it in, decides to call it Maisie and the cat makes herself at home on Andrew's bed.

Pamela Allen says: 'My books are made to SHARE. This creates the opportunity to ask questions, to anticipate, to discover and create.' Her first picture book, *Mr Archimedes' Bath* (Puffin Books, 1980) offers the person reading the book to a child to explain 'Archimedes Principle.' Archimedes was a Greek living in the 3rd century BC. He discovered the theory of water displacement. Legend has it that he made his discovery in the bath. Pamela Allen's Mr Archimedes shares his bath with a kangaroo, a goat and a wombat. His bath always overflows even when there is not much water in it.

Although this story can be instructional, it is also whimsical. 'The fun you have together is what it is all about,' says Pamela Allen. 'I have always seen my books as a fragment of theatre out there for you to dramatise and to make your own.'

Her books sometimes contain a subtle message. 'As the maker of picture books for the very young,' Pamela says, 'I use words and pictures to reveal meaning.'

In *Black Dog* (Hodder & Stoughton, 1991) Christina ignores her pet dog and dreams of a wonderful blue bird. Black Dog tries to

attract her attention by flying out of a tree. He falls and Christina takes him home.

> *She stroked his shiny black coat.*
> *She smelled his doggy smell.*
> *His heart was beating fast.*
> *Gently and carefully she wrapped him*
> *in the warmth of her body.*
> *'Black Dog,' she whispered, 'I love you.'*

Sometimes Pamela Allen uses rhyme to tell her story. The award-winning *Mr McGee Goes to Sea* (Puffin Books, 1992) begins:

> *Mr McGee was sipping tea*
> *beneath his spreading apple tree,*
> *when up above him in the sky*
> *a big black cloud came floating by.*

What adventures Mr McGee has when it rains so hard he floats out to sea! And he does not spill a single drop of tea from his teapot.

This is just one of many in the Mr McGee series. As with all the stories this one is charming, and the illustrations enchanting. Pamela Allen manages to capture mood and insight with the stroke of a brush.

Pamela Allen has won many prestigious awards in New Zealand, Australia and elsewhere. She is the first illustrator to have won the Children's Book Council of Australia Picture Book of the Year Award two years running with *Who Sank the Boat* – another story about animals, (1983) and *Bertie and the Bear*, (1984).

Pamela is a New Zealander but spent some years living in Australia where she earned a fine reputation. Meg Sorensen wrote: 'The characters in these books exude life, caught at the highest point of action and animated forever on the page...The picture books of Pamela Allen are very likely to be treasured by those who own them. They certainly have what it takes to join the ranks of enduring children's classics.'

Find out more about Pamela Allen on: http://www.bookcouncil. org.nz/writers/allenpamela.html

Or you might enjoy the interactive website http://english. unitechnology.ac.nz/nz/bookchat/current *The Potato People* by Pamela Allen is featured here.

Maurice Gee

Maurice Gee is one of New Zealand's foremost writers and he has written many books for older children.

Maurice Gee wrote his first children's novel in 1979. This was *Under the Mountain*, (Penguin, 1979). Although pure fantasy, this book has a real setting in Auckland, New Zealand's largest city which is built on a series of extinct volcanoes. Beneath these volcanoes are giant slugs, which plan to turn the world into a muddy playground for themselves by making the volcanoes, erupt. Two children, Rachel and Theo, are the only people able to stop this from happening. They have magic stones which will let them influence the minds of the slugs.

The battle between good and evil is a common theme in his science fiction novels. The trilogy *The Halfmen of O* (Oxford University Press, 1982) won the New Zealand Children's Book of the Year Award in 1983. The saga of the World of O continues with *The Priests of Ferris*, (Oxford University Press, 1984) and *Motherstone*, (Oxford University Press, 1985).

Maurice Gee was born in 1931 and spent much of his childhood in the Henderson area, west of Auckland City. Here as a boy he played in the Henderson Creek. Sometimes he would venture down the creek to its outlet in the Waitemata Harbour in a boat made from materials supplied by his father who was a carpenter.

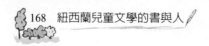

It was the creek, though, that held special significance. Here, Maurice Gee explains:

It was a place of marvellous and terrible things...I got my first sight of death. I'd run home from the creek to the safety and security of the kitchen, one the place of safety and affection, the other the place of adventure, danger, excitement...

This became the source for much of the material in his children's books. One book set at the creek is *The Fat Man*, (Penguin Books, 1994.) In this novel the Fat Man comes back to town to take revenge for being teased as a boy. Young Colin Potter, hungry because his father is out of work and the family has little food, stumbles on the Fat Man bathing in the creek. The Fat Man catches Colin stealing his chocolate and forces him to help steal some jewels. When the job is done...

'...here's your pay.' [The Fat Man] reached into his pocket and pulled out a shilling.
'No,' Colin said, but the fat man smiled.
'Take it, kid.' He closed Colin's fingers tightly on it. 'That makes you my accomplice. We robbed the old lady's house together. You went in didn't you, kid, and opened the window for me? ...So if I get caught, you get caught. We both go to prison. Now wouldn't that break your mother's heart?'
'Yes,' Colin sobbed.

From then on there is no escaping the Fat Man.

When people like Herbert Muskie take up residence in your mind there's nothing you can do to get them out. Time passing may push them back into the shadows, and daily events, happy events, dinners with meat and gravy, football matches at school, lock a door on them for a while. But they're always there...

Things become even tougher for Colin when he realises that it is his Dad the Fat Man is after. The Fat Man caused some controversy when it first appeared because it was so gritty and real. But it is certainly a book that once read is never forgotten.

Another feature common to many of the children's books is the era in which they take place. It is obviously the time of Maurice Gee's own childhood, during the Depression of the 1930s and the Second World War.

Some books are based on television series written by Maurice Gee. One such book is *The Fire-Raiser,* (Penguin Books, 1986). This book is set in 1915, earlier than the others. There is an arsonist in the small town of Jessop. Very early on the children have a fair idea who the culprit is, but they have a hard time convincing their parents and the police. One unusual character in this book is Miss Perez – a skeleton – who plays a crucial role in helping capture the *Fire-Raiser.*

Like most of Gee's story there are subtle lessons in *The Fire-Raiser.* Set during the First World War, it touches on blind patriotism and racial prejudice. Another book which examines the issue of racism is *The Champion*, set during the Second World War. An American serviceman comes to town. The children see a hero, a champion. Their parents see only a black man and must resolve their racist views before they can see him with the innocent eyes of the

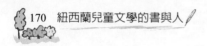

children. This is another book which developed out of a television series.

In 2002 Maurice Gee was awarded the Margaret Mahy Medal and Lecture Award by the Children's Literature Foundation for the tremendous contribution he has made to children's literature and literacy in New Zealand.

To learn more about Maurice Gee and his work go to: http://www.bookcouncil.org.nz/writers/geem.html

Dorothy Butler

Dorothy Butler did not start writing for children until she was in her mid-fifties. However she already had a considerable reputation, both in New Zealand and overseas, as an advocate for children's reading and literature. She has written several books for adults on the subject. *Cushla and her Books* about a multiple-handicapped child and the way books helped her adjust to life has been translated into Japanese and won Dorothy Butler awards in that country. It was also published in Taiwan.

Dorothy Butler established and ran a Reading Centre for children with reading problems and founded a bookshop which specialises in children's literature. She also worked for ten years as a children's editor for a publishing house. This last job came in handy when she decided to write her own stories. Normally the publisher will find an illustrator if the author does not illustrate her own work. But Dorothy's expertise in the area meant she knew the good illustrators and was able to choose the ones she wanted to work with.

She has won many awards in New Zealand and around the world. She says one of the good things about being a writer is, 'a lot of overseas travel when I was given awards…and visiting children in schools and libraries.'

Dorothy Butler's writing shows a close affinity with children and the way they think. This should not be too surprising, as she is the mother of eight children and grandmother to twenty-five.

Among my favourite books are the Brown Bear Barney series. They were first published as single titles, and in 1998 were combined into a collection (*My Brown Bear Barney*, Illustrated by Elizabeth Fuller, pub. Reed New Zealand.)

In the title story a little girl takes Barney, her bear, with her wherever she goes.　When she plays with her friend, Fred, she takes the bike, her old dog, two apples, her gumboots, *and* her brown bear Barney. He goes shopping with her, to bed, the beach and grandmother's. But, her mother tells her, Barney will not be able to go with her when she starts school. *We'll see about that*, the little girl thinks.

In the final of the three stories, Barney does go to school, but he has to stay out in the cloakroom. The class is preparing a performance for parents and friends and the little girl feels sorry for Barney stuck out on his own, in her satchel, hanging off the peg. Little does she know that Barney is actually out and about having an adventure of his own. In this book the pictures and words completely and wonderfully contradict each other.

Dorothy Butler obviously has a soft spot for bears. *Bears, Bears, Bears* is another book on the subject, as is *Hector, An Old Bear*, (Puffin, 1995). The illustrations in this book, beautifully done by Lyn Kriegler, show an early 20th century family whose daughter, Alexandra, has a much-loved bear called Hector. He has an accident and much as they try to fix him he can't be mended. So Alexandra's father buys her a new bear. Does she throws away Hector and take the new bear to bed with her? No! She gives the new bear to her brother and:

> *Then she lifted up her own bear,*
> *Her own bear, her own bear.*

When you have your own bear,
You do not need another.

The repeated phrases make this a simple but charming book to read to young children and the illustrations are full of detail that demonstrates the era – the cook in the kitchen, an old iron stove for her to bake in, the old-fashioned rocking horse.

Lulu, is also illustrated by Lyn Kriegler, (Hodder & Stoughton, 1990). Lulu is the neighbourhood stray cat. While the resident cats are spoilt and have little character, Lulu is *calm and courageous*. While the other cats are *eating fish, lapping milk...* Lulu finds her food in rubbish bins and stays *fresh as a daisy*.

Another book illustrated by Lyn Kriegler is *Higgledy Piggledy Hoddledy Hoy*, (Greenwillow Books, New York, 1991). This delightful story is built on made-up words.

Higgledy piggledy hobbledy hoy
A good little girl and a bad little boy...

Well, that's what the little girl thinks. When it is the boy's turn he goes:

Wiffley waffley widdledy wee
It's slow little you and fast little me...

But suddenly the band of animals following them shout, *STOP! WHAT ABOUT THE PICNIC?* As they munch their way through the delicious picnic the children stop arguing. The food is

For good little, fast little, wonderful US!

Dorothy Butler says as a child she was inspired by her mother and grandmother. 'My mother told us engrossing tales of her childhood. My grandmother who lived with us told us tales of coming to New Zealand in a sailing ship.'

She currently lives in The Old House at Karekare on the wild west coast of Auckland. Here she has a large children's library which is used by her grandchildren who live nearby as well as other children living in the small community.

Find out more about Dorothy Butler's interview on http://christchurchcitylibraries.com/Kids/ChildrensAuthors/DorothyButler.asp

Norman Bilbrough

Norman Bilbrough has been writing for thirty years and is a prize-winning author of adult stories, twice winning the *Sunday Star Times* Short Story Award. In 2000 he won the New Zealand section of the International PEN competition with *Hello Mr New Zealand* which draws on his experiences in Vietnamese refugee camps in Hong Kong during the 1980s. He also writes extensively for children and young adults.

Many stories have been published in the *School Journal* and there is a collection in *Dog Breath and Other Stories*, (Mallinson Rendell, 1998) which Norman Bilbrough describes as 'Yuk Realism'. Like many writers we have discussed in this series, he began his working life as a schoolteacher. He likes writing for children he says, 'because children demand simple stories with good plots. Children are closer to their imaginations than adult readers, so it's easier to grab them with strange tales, odd ways of looking at the world and crazy characters. I can use my imagination more directly and simply when I write for children.' His stories are, indeed, imaginative.

One such story is found in the novel, *The Birdman Hunts Alone*, (Penguin) which was shortlisted for the AIM Children's Book Awards in 1994. The story begins normally enough with three cousins on holiday together on a farm north of Auckland. It is not too long, though, before things change. Toby is mesmerised by the photograph of a woman in his bedroom. As he looks at the photo the woman, Eve, comes alive and speaks to him in his mind. She draws Toby, Rebecca and Sandra into her strange world, Zors, where she tells them of the legendary verse:

> *Three will wait in the fingers of stone*
> *The Birdman will come, hunting alone*
> *Five will return from the basin of lead*
> *Five will return from the river of the dead.*

Then she sends them on a quest across the many countries of Zors to find Arish's lost leader, Mandoc, who is the only one who can return Arish to the happy and just country it had once been. Their journey is dangerous and takes the three to many strange places such as Teeth in the Wind, the Towers of Silence. They overcome a force field and face up to the dreaded Riverman, but cannot find Mandoc. After many adventures they learn valuable lessons about their own strengths and weaknesses. In the end the prophetic verse comes true. Five do return with the Birdman who is actually none other than Mandoc.

The stories in *Dog Breath* are perfect evocations of adolescent boys and full of humour. They are *sometimes revolting, but always engaging...* as the blurb suggests. In the title story Matt gets the ideal job as a food taster for a Mr Shines. Matt gets hooked on the food and begins to put on weight. Another drawback is that he finds all the local dogs love him and his 'dog breath.' It turns out that the food he's been tasting is dog food. No wonder Norman Bilbrough calls the stories 'Yuk Realism.' One delightful secondary character in this story is Matt's father. He is introduced like this:

Then an old guy pressed his mouth against the glass and made a big wet smeary kiss.
'Come off it, Dad,' I mouthed.

In the same collection, *Mad Dad Disease* Mark's father left him when he was just two years old. Later he is forced to visit his father who is a vegetarian. Mark likes a nice, juicy steak and he tries to get out of the latest visit, but his mother insists she needs a break from his awful music. However, this time things are looking up. His father has a girlfriend who understands Mark and takes him horse riding. By the time Mark gets home even his mother has changed.

Many of the short stories deal with issues of the modern family, some of them quite weighty, but Norman Bilbrough manages a light touch. In *The Ghost of Katherine Mansfield*, Matt is unhappy because his mother has left home to live with a woman in another city. He skips school and meets the ghost of New Zealand's famous writer on a Wellington ferry. He takes her back to her old house in Tinakori Road, and she tells him about her life – and helps him solve his problems.

Another story dealing with the modern family is *Mosley's Dad* in which ten-year-old Mosley meets his Dad for the first time. Mosley is disappointed because he wanted his father to be a cool young guy. Instead his father is untidy and middle-aged. Then he discovers that his father likes cricket too. They arrange to have a game and Mosley feels a lot better about his Dad.

Norman Bilbrough says that his ideas often come from a feeling. "A feeling grabs me, or an idea.' One fanciful idea is *Mars Bar*. A strange kid called Mars Bar arrives at school. Jason befriends him but gets a fright when he discovers the kid eating electricity for his lunch. Mars Bar goes home after school in a flying saucer.

Norman Bilbrough lives in Wellington opposite the Otari Bush Reserve where the tuis wake him in the morning. Here he writes and works as a literary assessor.

Find out more about Norman Bilbrough on http://www. bookcouncil.org.nz/writers/bilbroughn.html

Fleur Beale

It was reported that J.K.Rowling did not use her full name when she wrote the Harry Potter series because boys don't read books by female authors, and she wanted boys to read her books. No such problem presented itself to Fleur Beale, even though her name is so obviously female with a name that is French for *flower*. Many of her books are aimed at boy readers and they love them.

Just look at some of the topics she writes about in her novels for teenagers -   In *Driving a Bargain*, (pub. Harper Collins, Auckland, 1994) a group of boys spend their summer holidays learning to drive an old wreck of a car around a paddock. Here Thomas has his first try:

> *That afternoon I got into the car first. I started it and didn't stall it! I hooned around the paddock, yelling and screaming. A corner! I flung the wheel to the right, then the left. A blip on the accelerator. I did something wrong and stalled it.*

This book was a finalist in the Junior Fiction category of the AIM Children's Book Awards, 1995 and it deals with a common theme explored by Fleur Beale – the need for teenagers to feel they belong.

Playing to Win (Scholastic, Auckland, 1999) is about New Zealand's favourite game – rugby football. Denny is new in town.

He feels left out, but would like to win the lovely Alice's attention and look good beside local boy Todd. He does make the rugby team, but things are not easy because he has responsibilities the others don't have. He has to help his mother out with the 'kids', his little twin sisters. He collects the twins from school and generally keeps an eye out for them. He allows them to jump all over him and tolerates their childish pranks. This is an endearing quality in Denny. One afternoon he has to take the kids to football practice.

> It took Todd about two second to find out I'd brought my twin sisters, and boy, did he hassle me. He baa-ed like a nanny goat. He called me Daddy. Then he called me Mummy. I didn't say anything. No way was I going to mess things up by losing my temper with Todd.
>
> ...I played on the wing, number eight, flanker and hooker...when a ruck went down, it was Todd's sprigs that left a pretty pattern on my back.
>
> The next time it was the elbow in the throat trick. I put my hand up and bent over coughing...
>
> "Denny! Denny! You're hurt!" The kids tore across the grass and threw themselves at me.
>
> "If he wasn't before, he will be now," Coach said...

Like so many of the authors we have discussed here Fleur Beale is a school teacher. She started writing children's stories for radio over twenty years ago. She says the best thing about being a writer is 'Being your own boss. Being able to make up a world of your own and then having adventures that perhaps you might never have in real life."

Fleur Beale does not only write for boys. Many of her books are written about girls. In *Lucky for Some* (pub. Scholastic, Auckland, 2002) Lacey Turner is forced to shift with her parents from the city into the country. The city has everything she wants, friends, dancing lessons, hairdressers, junk food, 'LIFE'. The country only offered a ramshackle new home, smelly cows, grass, rugby and 'NO LIFE'. But the nightmare does not quite come true. After a shaky start Lacey finds that country life isn't so bad after all. She makes friends – with a cow called Dancer – and learns how to take care of her. She practises leading Dancer around a ring ready for Agriculture Day at the school, but Dancer has a mind of her own. Miraculously, though, on the day Lacey leads Dancer around the ring perfectly.

If you're lucky, Fleur Beale says, ideas arrive out of the blue. Sometimes you have to dig deep to find them and sometimes they come from something that has happened. *Lucky for Some* was one such book. She explains how the story came about: 'Much of the background for *Lucky for Some* is based on the year we lived in a hundred-year-old cottage in the country while our house was being built. My daughters were twelve and ten and they had a calf and a goat for Agriculture Day. The calf, like Lacey's would not lead; she was dreadful. But on the day, for some reason, she behaved perfectly and won the cup for leading.'

In 1999 Fleur Beale was the Writer in Residence at the Dunedin College of Education and the same year she received an Honour Award from the New Zealand Post Children's Book Awards for her novel, *I Am Not Esther*, the story of a girl trying to cope with her new life in a fundamentalist Christian family. In 2003 this book was reprinted with new cover. Fleur Beale was inspired to write this book when one of her students was banished from his family for going against their religious principles.

All together Fleur Beale has written 13 novels for teenagers. These novels stay with you long after you've read them. It is no wonder that she has such a strong appeal with teenagers.

Find out more about Fleur Beale on: http://www.bookcouncil. org.nz/writers/bealefleur.html

---

Martin Baynton

Martin Baynton was born in London, England in 1953 and came to New Zealand to live when he was thirty-four. He is a versatile writer who writes books and stories for children and adults as well as scripts for stage, television and radio. Not only does he write books for children, he also illustrates both his own and the work of others. He is also an actor for television and the theatre.

The earliest influence on Martin Baynton was A.A.Milne and Winnie the Pooh series. His love of reading as a child encouraged him to become a writer. 'Writers were my heroes,' he says. The best part of being a writer, he says, is being your own boss. But it can be lonely sometimes.

As well as illustrating books for other authors he writes his own stories and we will look at some of his books here which feature dragons and dinosaurs.

There has been a lot of controversy about gold mining on the Coromandel where Martin Baynton lives, so it is small wonder that *Under the Hill* (Scholastic New Zealand, 1996) is a heavily disguised morality story about the evils of strip mining for gold. The miners came in…

> *Dozers, loaders,*
> *diggers too,*
> *tore and dug*

And spat and blew.
They dug the rock
where, snug and still,
something slumbered
under the hill...

The rock was hard, the rock was old,
the rock was guarding precious gold.

They stole the hilltop,
day by day,
they took the gold...
and drove away.

The 'something that slumbered' was a creature that looked like a miniature dragon. He woke, hungry for his staple diet, gold. So he left his hill and went out looking for something to eat. He stole gold from people as they slept, from divers on 'sunken wrecks', from the church and mosque, from teeth fillings, from the bank. In short from anywhere he could find it.

Finally the people had had enough. They asked the creature for their gold back and he agreed as long as the people replaced his hill with the gold inside. Instead they created a plastic hill, and the deal was off.　All is well that ends well, though, and the creature finally made a place of beauty out of another mountain and this one was covered with golden buttercups.

A series that has a strong feminist slant is about Jane who was a knight. In *Jane and the Dragon* (Scholastic New Zealand, 1988) Jane did not like sewing. She did not want to become a lady-in-waiting. She wanted to be a knight, but:

Her father laughed.
'What nonsense,' he said. 'Only boys can become knights.'

Jane told everybody that she wanted to be a knight and they all laughed. The only person to take her seriously was the court jester and he helped her train as a knight. Then one day a dragon stole the prince. Dressed as a knight Jane rushed off to save the prince. She...

followed the dragon to his mountain lair.
'Release the boy!' she demanded in her sternest voice.
The dragon laughed...

A terrible fight ensued. Both Jane and the dragon got close to killing each other, but they did not follow it through. When Jane asked the dragon why he didn't kill her, he said it was because he did not like hurting people.

Then why did you steal the prince?
Because it is expected of me.
'Then do the unexpected,' said Jane.

She then revealed to the dragon that she was a girl, and they made friends. Jane agreed to visit the dragon every Saturday. On her return to the palace with the prince the king and queen were very grateful, but mystified about the strange knight. When they realised that it was Jane, the king thanked her by making her a proper knight - with Saturdays off.

In *The Dragon's Purpose* (Ashton Scholastic, 1990) Jane, the knight, found the dragon very miserable on one of her Saturday visits.

He did not have a purpose in life because he no longer scared people. He loved Saturdays, naturally, but the rest of the week was dreary because he had nothing to do. Jane was worried. She asked her friend, the court jester, what to do but he did not know. She asked the court wizard, but he was too busy trying out a new rain-making spell because it had not rained for a long time.　Then she came up with a solution. The dragon could frighten the people in the Hallowe'en parade. This worked well, but it was only temporary, and, the dragon said:

> '...it was a sham; a piece of theatre. Thank you for trying to help, but this was never my purpose. I'm not an entertainer.' And he flew away without saying goodbye.

Finally the dragon came up with his own solution that did not scare anyone and helped the king and his people.

> 'See that!" bellowed the dragon. "I scared the rain right out of it [the cloud]. I'm a giant green dragon born to scare rain clouds.'

Martin Baynton lives in Whangamata on the Coromandel Peninsula where he spends his time writing and riding his horse.

Find out more about Martin Baynton on: http://www.bookcouncil. org.nz/writers/bayntonmartin.html

Jack Lasenby

Award-winning children's author, Jack Lasenby, was not always a writer. During the 1950s he worked in bush country trapping possums and shooting deer. However, like so many of the other writers featured here he later became a school teacher, and later still taught English at Wellington Teachers College.

His first novel, *The Lake* (Oxford University Press, Auckland, 1987) is the story of thirteen-year-old Ruth who runs away from home to escape her step-father who keeps trying to molest her. She heads for the lake where she spent her holidays before her father died. It is a long journey, but Ruth gains strength and self-knowledge from it. As with many of Jack Lasenby's books the issues explored here are real and life for the protagonist is often challenging.

Similarly in *The Mangrove Summer*, (Oxford University Press, Auckland, 1988), winner of the prestigious Esther Glen Medal, adventure turns to disaster. In this book set in the 1940s Jack Lasenby draws on his own experiences as a child. He spent his childhood holidays with three cousins at a bay on the Coromandel Peninsula. 'Our father and the cousins' mother were dead,' he said, 'so we made a sort of intact family each summer.' George, the protagonist, his little brother Jimmy, his bossy sister Jill and their cousins hide in the bush to escape an invasion by the Japanese, but the story takes a tragic turn when the two youngest boys in the party go missing.

We found Derek first. It had rained all night. Jill and Graham took the dinghy and rowed away in the dark. We left a stew in the camp oven and followed the mouth of the creek. As the light came up, the punt skimmed over the mud downriver...

Three channels on, Ann heard him. She was over the side of the punt, half swimming, half wading, before I saw him sitting on a tiny dry patch among the mangroves, the tide about his feet. It was his whimpers Ann heard because he couldn't call out. He couldn't even lift his arms to her... 'Where's Jimmy?' she asked, cuddling Derek in the stern.

'There,' he whispered... 'Back there.' It was all he could say. He didn't seem to recognise us.

Far from real life is the setting of *The Conjuror*, (Oxford University Press, Auckland, 1992) a compelling read about a brutal futuristic society where the social order is dictated by sex and eye colour. Johnny is a Grey who is captured and sent to work in Moory for a family of Browns. Prejudice, ignorance, brutality and revenge are all explored here but balanced by Johnny's warm relationships with Hemmy who treats him like a son, the Brown girl from the next-door farm and her father, Thomas who enlightens him:

The past used to be a vague time before the Punishment. Now, Thomas spoke of time that spread so far back it filled me with fear. I resisted most such new ideas...and was forced into making judgements, taking decisions. Suddenly I was in a world of light...

... 'We are a small part of the whole world,' he said. 'After the Punishment, as they call it, the Sisters built a system of

slavery based on sex and eye colour. That's what I think must have happened. The Mother Goddess, the Punishment, the Conjuror, the sin of being a Blue, humbug! All humbug!'

Among my favourite Jack Lasenby books are the short story collections, the *Uncle Trev* series and *The Lies of Harry Wakatipu* (Longacre, 2000). The latter was short-listed for the 2001 New Zealand Post Children's Book Awards, and again, the setting is based on Jack Lasenby's own experience:

When I ran away from home I went deer culling...Deer were a curse in the bush, and the government paid a handful of tough jokers to shoot them out. But that is where the reality ends. Harry Wakatipu is a pack horse. *He's mean, he pongs, and he tells lies...* And he tells fantastic stories, but he has met his match in Wiki the storytelling dog.

> *'Nowadays,' said Wiki, 'kids ride horses to school. In the olden days we rode elephants. Every school had an elephant paddock...'*
> *'Huh!'*
> *'There were twenty-one kids in our family. We sat on our elephant in single file with our legs sticking out...'*
> *'Huh!'*
> *'Our elephant's name was Portugal...'*
> *'Huh!'*
> *'Harry Wakatipu, I wish you'd stop saying, "Huh!" I can't remember what I'm going to say next.'*
> *'Huh!'*

If the truth be known Wiki, is as big a liar as Harry, but she is good at housework.

In 2002 the first of a series of books about Aunt Effie was published. Fanciful, but again set in the area Jack Lasenby loves so well, the kauri forests of Coromandel, the Aunt Effie series tell of her six huge pig-hunting dogs, her twenty-six nephews and nieces, their adventures in the forest and their battles with the pirates of Hauraki Gulf.

Jack Lasenby has been frequently honoured for his writing, winning many awards and fellowships. He claims that is favourite food is, 'Everything from huhu grubs to ice cream...' He lives as close as the sea as possible, just above the high water mark at Paremata, north of Wellington, where he sails 'the most beautiful dinghy in the world.'

Find out more about Jack Lasenby on: http://www.bookcouncil.org.nz/writers/lasenby.html

Four Rising Stars

So far we have discussed many prize-winning New Zealand children's authors. In this chapter we will look at four rising stars – the new breed of talented writers.

Deborah Burnside's first novel, *On a Good Day,* (Penguin, 2004) is the story of Lee whose mother is an alcoholic and whose father is something of a mystery. It is a rich novel with a cast of utterly believable characters. Hinemoa, the girl across the road who models Lee's wearable art entry; Evie who lives next door and offers Lee a haven from the uproar of her life. Gunna, Lee's *secret crush*, is not only drop-dead gorgeous, but also understanding:

> *'Lee.' He looks at my knees, at a spot above my head, and down at his own chest. 'When you spoke at the funeral about Albert I was really proud of you...Now you sound angry and bitter and not at all like the person I really admired yesterday. Your mother made a mistake...'*

Deborah has always been determined to be a writer. Although this is her first novel she has had short stories published. She writes for both adults and children. *On a Good Day* was written with the help of the New Zealand Society of Authors mentor programme. Deborah's mentor was Tessa Duder who has been discussed in these pages.

High Tide by Anna Mackenzie (Scholastic New Zealand, 2003) was featured in the Children's Literature Foundation Notable Books of 2003. Sam (short for Samantha) Edmonds puts her name down to go on a school tramping trip. You just know that it is not going to turn out well because the novel opens:

> *If we'd known how things would turn out, none of us would have signed up in the first place. But then they say it's always easy to see in hindsight what you would have done differently. And I guess none of it would have happened if we hadn't all been hankering for a bit of adventure.*

And things do go terribly wrong. This is an action-packed drama. It is well written and tightly paced. 'Teenagers are discovering themselves and their world,' Anna says. 'They are dealing with issues and emotions that are new, finding a way to grow into the adults they will become. I enjoy that as a context to my writing.' One reviewer says of *High Tide* that is a 'really very good adventure thriller…It is a very good novel.'

Also with an outdoor theme is Mary Barrow's novel (*Rough, Tough and Had Enough*) published by Scholastic. Here we meet Michael who is taken tramping by his father, despite his protests. They meet a hunter who appears unfriendly but Michael learns a lot about bush craft from him and (inadvertently) about father-son relationships. When his father is injured, it is up to Michael to use his initiative and as a result he gains the hunter's respect and friendship.

Mary has a keen eye for detail, and is obviously familiar with the terrain and setting of the story. After a day's hard slog Michael and his father make it to an overnight hut and…

...when I lay down, every muscle in my body relaxed. The crackle and hiss of the dying fire was the only sound and the silence in the hut was weird...I was cuddling into my warm, soft sleeping bag when I heard the rain start. It sounded soft and gentle, like a lullaby. I snuggled further into my downy cocoon waiting for the gentle pitter-patter to put me to sleep. Instead the heavens burst without warning. The rain hit the iron roof like machine gun bullets...The wind picked up and soon the whole shack was shuddering as if it was about to be launched into orbit.

Adele Broadbent's *Wee Jack* is loosely based on the life of her grandfather. Wee Jack is fifteen and excited about beginning his career as an apprentice jockey. Adele researched the novel thoroughly. After a visit to a race track before dawn on a cold, dark winter's day she says, 'Feeling, smelling, hearing your scenes' settings makes it so much easier to write them. Not being a horse person, I wanted to experience the track as my grandfather had...No gloves, scarves or hats to ward off the icy air...I listened to the light birdsong in contrast to the horses' hooves thundering past me on the track...Without my morning at the track, I could never have written the relevant scenes.'

Here is how Adele put that research to work in *Wee Jack*:

Just as we reached the rail circling the course, Kenny cantered past on Dazzle. I'd always loved to watch a horse run, their huge muscles powering them along, and their tails flowing out behind.

My most favourite thing in the world was to ride – fast. With the wind in my face and the sound of hooves pounding a rhythm beneath me. Feeling like part of the horse.

I rested my chin on the rail. All I'd managed to ride so far was a bicycle.

'When do you gallop them?' I asked.

'Each horse is at different stages depending on the next race,' said Mr Mac, not taking his eyes off Dazzle...Kenny brought Dazzle in after her three laps. Her coat was wet with sweat, her eyes large and excited.

All four authors live in the Hawkes Bay area and are married with children.

Gwenda Turner (1947-2001)

Gwenda Turner was born in Australia. When she left school at 16 she became a secretary and three years later she moved to New Zealand where she completed a Graphic Design course at Wellington Polytechnic. After a stint on Norfolk Island running a handcraft studio and working as a Graphic Design consultant, she moved back to New Zealand and married John Turner in 1974. She spent the rest of her life in Christchurch.

Her first book, *Akaroa: Banks Peninsula, New Zealand* was published three years later and shortly after that she began writing and illustrating for children. *The Tree Witches*, (Penguin 1983) won the Russell Clark Award for illustrations in 1984 and the Australian Children's Book of the Year Award for best picture book in 1985. Since then she has had nearly thirty books published, all of them much-loved by the children who read them.

Her style is realistic and features children in typical New Zealand settings. 'My style is true to life,' she said, 'and I research everything I draw.' Several of the books are educational, such as *New Zealand A,B,C*, (Penguin 1985), *New Zealand 1, 2, 3* (Penguin 1986), *Over on the Farm* (Penguin, 1993), and *Farm* Animals, (Penguin 1995). They might be instructional, but they are also fun.

Over on the farm
Where the small fish dive

Lived an old mother frog
And her little tadpoles
Five
Swim said the mother
We swim said the five
So they swam all day
Where the small fish dive.

Many of Gwenda Turner's books are based on true stories. She said: 'I like to base my stories on real events, real children and real animals I've met. I like to use reality – a real remembered moment.' *The Builder's Cat*, (Penguin 1999) is based on Abraham, a real cat who goes to work with Mr Couper, a builder. Abraham likes to explore. He gets in the wheelbarrow, climbs trees, and investigates buckets and watering cans. He doesn't mind, at all, the noises around him, like the buzz of the drill and the banging of Mr Couper's hammer.

There are no strong storylines. Rather each book tells of those 'remembered moments'. *The Ferry Ride* (Penguin, 1998) is about an exciting day out for a little boy and his father. The travel on the Interislander, the ferry which runs between the North and the South Islands. They watch cars and trucks being loaded, they watch the ship sail away from the wharf and count the seagulls following alongside. The sea air makes them hungry so they go to the cafeteria for hot chips and best of all they visit the Captain on the bridge. The captain lets the little boy wear his hat.

Dad and I had a great view from the bridge of the ship. Land ahoy! I cried.

My favourite book is *Penny and Pocket* (Penguin 2001) which tells the true story of a tiny stray kitten who is found on the side of the road. It is so small it fits into a pocket and that's how it got its name. Penny is a Jack Russell dog and Penny loves Pocket at first sight.

Penny thinks Pocket is her baby. She picks Pocket up carefully in her mouth, just like a mother cat.

Sadly Gwenda Turner died in 2001, but her legacy to the children of New Zealand and the world are the many books she wrote and illustrated.

For find out more about Gwenda Turner go to: http://christchur chcitylibraries.com/Kids/FamousNewZealanders/Gwenda.asp

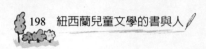

Paula Boock

Paula Boock is a novelist for young adults. She was born in Dunedin and after her education at the University of Otago she worked as an editor for publishers John McIndoe. In 1995 she went to Longacre Press where she became a part-owner.

Her writing has received recognition in a number of ways. In 1991 she was awarded a grant from the Queen Elizabeth II Arts Council (now Creative New Zealand)). Three years later she became the writing fellow at Dunedin College of Education. In 1992 her first novel, *Out Walked Mel* won the AIM Best First Book Award and was a finalist for the Esther Glen Medal. Her second novel won the Esther Glen Medal for the Best New Zealand Children's Book in 1994. She also held the Robert Burns Fellowship at the University of Otago in 1999.

Home Run (Longacre, 1995) was a finalist in the senior section of the 1996 AIM Children's Book Awards. In it Bryony Page is the new girl in class. She has come from Christchurch to a multi-cultural school in Auckland and feels decidedly out of place. The only people she seems to be able to make friends with are the quiet girls in class – 'the wimps' as the others call them. But Bryony wants to be with the in-crowd and she is not easily defeated. There is one thing she knows she can shine at – softball. Her old team in Christchurch had been provincial champions. But when she gets her chance to show what she can do she is nervous:

Suddenly, too late, she realised the ball was through her, whizzing on to the park fence for an automatic home run. Bryony couldn't believe it. She stopped where she was…She never missed ones as simple as that.

Still she doesn't fit in. Then she learns to act like the tough kids who appear to despise her. Just how far is she prepared to go to be one of them?

They didn't usually wag school two days in a row, but the next day Mr Kirk was away sick and everyone in H10 was pretending to be someone else to confuse the relieving teacher.

Things get even trickier:

There was a sign in one corner of the shop. Shoplifitng is a crime. Offenders will be prosecuted…She found a couple of tapes she knew Shel would like, and slowly lowered them under the line of the shelf. Then she placed them carefully in the undone section of her school pack…

A special friendship with Ata begins to blossom, but that creates a difficulty of its own. Bryony comes from a well-off family, Ata's family are poor. Bryony is white, Ata is a Maori. *Home Run* is typical of Paula Boock's style with a feisty female protagonist, realistic setting and socially relevant situation.

The 1997 novel, *Dare Truth or Promise* was shortlisted for the 1998 New Zealand Post Children's Book Awards. Louie and Willa meet at the Burger Giant where they both work, but their lives are very different. Louie is a prefect at school, a model student who intends going to university to become a lawyer. Willa, on the other hand, was expelled from her high school for having a relationship with a fundamentalist preacher. She lives in a pub and just wants to study quietly to become a chef, but she had not reckoned on Louie coming into her life and changing it forever.

Power & Chaos was published in 2000. It is based on a futuristic television series called, *The Tribe*. A police state is established when a virus begins killing off all the adults in New Zealand. Martin's mother gets ill:

> *That weekend she was admitted to the hospital. I don't know how to write about that time. Mum said all the right things, she smiled at us and talked brightly, but it was there written all over her face...VIRUS. The lines, the hollowed eyes, the rapidly sinking face – we stood over her in our stupid ugly masks and we all knew we were watching Mum's last days.*

Martin suddenly finds himself with more to worry about than being jealous of Bray, his successful older brother, or impressing schoolmate Trudi Taylor. But this is not 'one of those fruity teenage books with a happy ending.' It is said that power corrupts and absolute power corrupts absolutely. Martin realises that with all the adults dying of the virus, the young are now in charge. He becomes Zoot, steely-eyed leader of the new order – power and chaos.

Paula Boock lives in Wellington, where she writes for television. Find out more about her on: http://www.bookcouncil.org.nz/writers/boock.html

Janice Marriott

Janice Marriott was born in England and moved to New Zealand with her family when she was eleven. She went to high school in Gisborne and Napier and following her studies at Victoria University in Wellington she became a librarian. She travelled to America and Canada where she worked in radio and television. Later, back in New Zealand, she became a teacher and began writing for children in the 1980s. In 1994 she was the inaugural writer-in-residence at the Auckland College of Education.

Her novels are realistic and mostly humorous. *Crossroads* is an exception. This novel for young adults is more serious, dealing as it does, with death and grieving. It won the Aim Supreme Award and the Senior Fiction Award in 1996.It has been described as a 'compelling exploration of two teenagers in crisis deepened by metaphor and literary resonances, especially echoes from Hamlet.' Janice Marriott herself describes it as being 'about the responsibilities of being a driver.'

'I write,' she says, 'funny books about how difficult it is for children to understand adults.' *Brain Drain* (Ashton Scholastic, 1993) is one such book. The protagonist, Henry Jollifer's mother tells him she is thinking of selling their house. Despondent, he watches television:

A politician was telling us that 25,000 New Zealanders emigrated last year which was like the whole of Timaru disappearing..."It was the cream of our young people". He called it the "brain drain". I sat up.

"What's he mean by a brain drain?"

"Oh, [Henry's mother replied] it's when the brainiest people leave the country."

"But-but...why didn't you tell me before!"

I'd never realised countries were like clothes – there were cool and uncool ones...

I rushed to my bedroom which in times of crisis doubles as my office. Less brilliant people would have panicked, but I managed to do what great businessmen do. I grabbed hold of all the problems of my present life...and time-travelled them into the future. This is called Planning Ahead...all the problems of my life could be solved by one daring plan...I couldn't stop Mum selling our house but I could stop her encouraging me to take up a career as a street kid. I could emigrate! I could join the brain drain.

There is only one small problem. Henry just has to find the money for the airfare. Make that two small problems – he has only got a month in which to do it. *Brain Drain* is one of a trilogy. The other two books about the amazing Henry Jollifer are *Letters to Lesley* (1989 and *Kissing Fish*, 1997.

'I like writing books about the extraordinary in ordinary daily life,' Janice Marriott says. 'I like to see the world through fresh eyes, and that is what a child does. I like the energy of children and their sense of humour and that is also something I put in my writing.' One of my favourite books, *Hope's Rainbow*, exemplifies all of this.

Hope's life is turned upside-down when her mother takes her and her two brothers to live in the city – leaving their Dad behind – and all because of an argument over the vet. Hope just cannot understand it. She hates living in the city. She hates having to be responsible for her little brother, Fred. She misses her goat and life on the farm and is worried about her dog, Bunsen. Bunsen is used to life in the country and he has as much trouble as Hope in adapting to city life. As if all this is not bad enough, she is worried about her mother who doesn't seem to do anything much except slump in front of the telly. Hope decides to cheer her mother up by organising a surprise birthday party for her. But a fire interrupts her plans, and Hope gets a much better party than she could have ever wished for.

Janice Marriott has a wonderfully luxuriant garden at the back of the central Wellington cottage where she now lives, so it is no surprise that she was asked to write some gardening books as part of the Yates Gardening for Kids series. Yates is a company that markets seeds and plants for the home gardener, and they have a very popular gardening book for adults. In *Gardening for Kids* (Harper Collins, 2002) illustrated by Elena Petrov, there is advice on soil types, making compost, garden pests and garden friends. Among the garden friends are the praying mantis and lady birds which eat the aphids who suck the juices out of roses; bees which collect nectar to make honey and pollinate flowers and worms who help make soil rich and full of nutrients.

Growing Things to Eat, (Harper Collins, 2003) again cleverly illustrated by Elena Petrov, shows how to create a herb garden, how to read a seed packet, and how to make a scarecrow. It talks about the garden's buried treasure – those root vegetables that hide their food underground, like carrots and potatoes. There is even advice on

how to grow your own name on a pumpkin, how to grow a cucumber
in a jar and how to cultivate your own food without a garden.

Find out more about Janice Marriott on: http://www.bookcouncil.
org.nz/writers/marriott.html

Ron Bacon (1924-2005)

Ron Bacon was born in Australia in 1924 and moved to New Zealand when he was seven years old. He became a school teacher, as so many of the authors we have discussed have done, and he saw a need for children's books about Maori legends. In this way he was in the forefront of the revival of Maoritanga in New Zealand. Prior to this the culture of 20th century New Zealand was predominantly European. Maori children were actively discouraged from speaking Maori and very little Maori culture was taught in schools.

His first book was *The Boy and the Taniwha* published in 1966. It was the first of its kind, illustrated by a well-known Maori artist and carver, Para Matchitt. Other titles followed with a similar focus on Maori folklore including *Hautupatu and the Bird Woman* (1979); *The House of the People* (1977), and *The Fish of Our Fathers* (1984) which won the Picture Book Award of 1985.

One of the outstanding books in this series is *Rua and the Sea People*, (Waiatarua Publishing, 1968) again illustrated by Para Matchitt. Rua, a little Maori boy lived in a coastal village and loved to sit with his grandmother and watch the sea '…twinkling as if it had caught all the stars that shone on warm summer nights.' Best of all he liked watching the fishermen as they paddled their canoes out into the bay. In time Rua grew old enough to learn the ways of the men – how to bait a fishing hook, how to become a warrior and do the haka (war dance). One day a thing, big and tall appeared in the bay.

The people ran from the cooking fires and across the marae and they looked out from the hill, and there, coming across the bay, was a small canoe, and in the canoe, the Turehu, the fairy folk!

In spite of the fact that Rua was afraid of the 'fairy folk' he joined the other warriors as they went out to chase the intruders away.

But the leader of the Turehu lifted his hand and spoke words, and then he did a dreadful thing. The Turehu, awful with his pale skin and pale eyes, stepped close to Rua. And Rua trembled...and said, 'Go from here, you Turehu! ...Please go and leave me...to look after my grandmother!

But the Turehu did not hurt Rua. He gave him a nail and Rua saw that it might have many uses. As you might have guessed, the Turehu were not the fairy folk, but were in fact the first Europeans to arrive in New Zealand.

One of the interesting aspects of this book is the method of illustration. The art work is impressionistic, with the pictures created out of patterns of curves, squares or triangles. The artist explains: 'The early Maori people had no written language; they wrote their stories as carvings or as paintings, or made weavings patterns that told a story. [Some] patterns...curve and flow like the coils of the unfolding fern, or surge like rising waves.'

Ron Bacon did not only write about ancient legends, he also had an eye on modern life as his Hemi series shows. *Hemi, the Skateboard and Susquatch Harrison*, (1992) illustrated by Richard Hoit is one of my favourites. Hemi's Uncle Pookey sends him a skateboard from Hong Kong. *It was shiny green and hot pink, with matching pink wheels and a bent-up end. The helmet was pink too, and the packet of socks weren't socks at all – they were pads to wear on his knees and elbows.*

When Hemi goes to the netball courts at school which is the best place to ride, all the other children are watching Susquatch Harrison who is 'practising handstanding on his old dinged-up board – the Harrison Special, he called it.' The children gather around Hemi to admire his new skateboard and Susquatch joins them.

> *Susquatch looked at the board, then slowly, softly he rubbed it against his face, feeling its smooth green and yellow shine. He said, "Cool, real cool!" and Hemi felt good, for he knew this wasn't the way Susquatch usually talked to people as small as he was.*

Susquatch tries out Hemi's skateboard and then he shows Hemi some moves such as the 'kerbie' and 'kick turn'.

> *And Hemi laughed and put his foot on his board, ready to ride, and he said, 'Cool, man! Real cool!'*

At the end of the book is a useful list of safety suggestions for children using skateboards.

Ron Bacon's books are just too many to record here. *The Naming of the Land,* illustrated by Manu Smith (Waiatarua Publishing, 1998) was shortlisted in the non-fiction section of The New Zealand Post Children's Book Awards in 1999. This is a fascinating story about Maori place names; the ancient stories, the meanings, and the wisdom of the tohunga (priest) as he names the places in our land. This is also a good book to help work out the meanings of other Maori place names. Another title *Surf Lifesaving,* photographed by Anthony Heath, was shortlisted in 2003.

Ron Bacon died in 2005 after a long career and even today over fifty of Ron Bacon's books are still in print. In 1994 he was justly awarded the Children's Literature Association Award for Services to Children's Literature in recognition of his long and distinguished career as a writer for children.

Find out more about Ron Bacon on: http://www.bookcouncil. org.nz/writers/baconron.html

New Zealand Post Book Awards for Children and Young Adults

Every year there is a national festival celebrating the New Zealand Post Book Awards for Children and Young Adults. Readings, author talks, an on-line quiz, face-painting, the opportunity to make and fly a kite and create a beach mural are just some of the activities offered for children to participate in. Many of the finalists (and ultimate winners) are writers we have discussed in this book and I thought it fitting that for the final chapter we would take a look at these awards. In doing so we shall meet up with some old friends.

Many old favourites have been short listed. David Hill was shortlisted for *Coming Back*, (Mallinson Rendel, 2004) a young adult novel about teenagers involved in a car crash. Ken Catran was in the same category for *Robert Moran – Private* (Lothian Books, 2004), a novel about a soldier in the Second World War. Fleur Beale had two books in the Junior fiction. One was *A New Song in the Land* (Scholastic, 2004), set in 1840 when the Maori protagonist Atapo escapes slavery at the hands of her enemies. The other is in a quite different style. *Walking Lightly* tells the story of Millie who, although her parents are rich and she could have all the stuff she wants, is not interested. She would rather walk lightly through the world. Gavin Bishop was in the Picture Book section with four beautifully illustrated Maori myths in *Taming the Sun*, (Random House, 2004).

As you see there are several categories in the awards. The Junior Fiction Award went to Jack Lasenby for *Aunt Effie and the Island That Sank,* (Longacre Press, 2004). This, the third, in the Aunt Effie series is just as crazy as the earlier books. Aunt Effie becomes restless, so she and her 26 nieces and nephews are off again on a treasure hunt across the pirate-infested Hauraki Gulf. Meanwhile back in Auckland One Tree Hill has sprung a leak and Rangitoto Island is sinking while the Prime Minister gambles away the nation's taxes in the Casino Tower.

The winner of the Children's Choice Award went to another author we have met - Lynley Dodd. *The Other Ark*, (Mallinson Rendel, 2004) is both written and illustrated by this ever-popular author. In it Noah's Ark is packed and ready to sail, but there are still plenty of animals to be saved. Sam Jam Balu is asked to fill Ark Number Two and he knows exactly what needs to be done. But Sam has his work cut out for him as he tries to coax an extraordinary selection of creatures on board, including the armory dilloes, the pom-pom palavers and the blunderbuss dragons.

The Non-Fiction Award was won by poet, Gregory O'Brien, with his *Welcome to the South Seas: Contemporary New Zealand Art For Young People* (Auckland University Press, 2004). This is a vivid introduction to contemporary New Zealand art and a lesson in how to engage with art. Over 45 artists are discussed and represented by at least one piece of their work. In this way the book takes in some of the liveliest creations of the last 30 years.

Bernard Beckett, a relative new-comer, but prolific writer, won the Young Adult Fiction Award with his controversial book, *Malcolm and Juliet*, (Longacre Press, 2004). Malcolm is sixteen. With the mind of a scientist, the body of a teenager, and an ambition to reconcile the two, he decides that this year for the Science Fair he will make a documentary – on sex.

Winner of the Picture Book Award and the overall winner was Kate De Goldi with *Clubs: A Lolly Leopold Story*, (Trapeze, 2004) illustrated by Jacqui Colley. Lolly Leopold's teacher, Ms Love, is a glorious creature. She has a tuatara (big lizard) tattoo and a long ponytail that she swings like a lasso. Almost the whole class is involved in at least one club or another. Each has its own rules but Lolly isn't that impressed. It's not long before there are only three people in Room 7 not in a club. Ms Love has promised Lolly that she'll play her trumpet at Grandparent's Day if she tells the Clubs story.

The judges said of *Clubs*: 'This is a book that almost introduces a new genre, a book that Margaret Mahy has described as a breakthrough in New Zealand publishing. This book won because it did more than carefully explore known territory. It showed us new ways to tell stories, new ways to use pictures, and new ways to mix the words and pictures together. The voice of Lolly Leopold was so real and the world of the Tai Tapu school playground so convincing that we forgot all about the grown-ups with their names on the cover.'

It was another wonderful year for children's literature and I hope you have enjoyed reading about just a few of the authors and illustrators who keep children in New Zealand and around the world well-informed and happily entertained.

Find out more about the awards and the authors on: http://christchurchcitylibraries.com/Kids/LiteraryPrizes/NZPost/

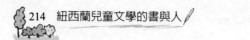

Appendix I

World Chinese Writers' Association
Fifth Global Conference---Taipei, March 2003
New Zealand Writing and Writers:
A Reflection of Many Cultures
An address by William Taylor,
National President, New Zealand
Society of Authors (Pen New Zealand Inc.)

Kia Ora (Maori greeting)

Your invitation to me to be present for this, your fifth global conference, is a significant honour that you have graciously extended to the New Zealand Society of Authors (PEN NZ Inc). It is an exceptionally generous gesture on your part. All members of our society join with me in expressing good wishes to you all and in expressing a hope that the bonds of fellowship and friendship already established between the Oceania Chinese Writers' Association and ourselves be further developed and cemented. This is not an idle or empty wish. While the differences that exist in the aims and compositions of our two societies should be recognised, it is those things that we have in common as writers and that bind us together that give us the building blocks for an even more significant partnership. I am, of course, enormously impressed that so many of you have made the effort to attend this conference - and from so many places around the world.

When I spoke at the 2nd Oceania Conference of Chinese writers in 2001, I said then that it mattered little whether we were writers in Mandarin Chinese, English, French, Danish . . . or indeed in any other language, we all shared the same anxieties as writers, and lived in the hope that we may better reflect aspects of the world in which we all live, of how we live in that world, and relationships between people. I said that then. I say it again today; I do believe that it bears repeating.

New Zealand writing is indeed a reflection of many cultures and our traditions of writing have been brought from many points of the globe and, over the short span of one and a half centuries of colonisation have melded into the distinctive 'voice' we have today. The provision of a written language in the early 19th century to our indigenous people, the Maori, and the emergence since that time of Maori writers has further added to and enriched that 'voice'. Early European settlement, primarily from the British Isles but also from many other mainly northern European countries provided the initial foundations for the building of our literature. Among those early arrivals there were, obviously, writers and printers - people to whom the written word was precious and of importance. The rich oral tradition of the Maori was very soon to be reflected in our early literature. We are, of course, no longer a completely 'euro-centric' nation. The forces of history as well as of geography have seen to that. Migration to our islands was always diverse and, today, that diversity is even more marked. We have increasingly significant populations of Chinese people, Indian people, peoples from the tiny Pacific Ocean dots of Polynesia, Melanesia and Micronesia, and, as often dictated by world events as for any other reason, respectably sized communities of those from south east Asian nations, the Middle East and from Africa - both north and south. As many of you here today will know, from the earliest days of settlement, Chinese people have been a significant presence in our national society. In the days when I was teaching in the region where I live, the central North Island of New Zealand, I taught many Kiwi kids of Chinese descent whose forebears settled the land well over a hundred years ago. In recent years, of course, a far greater diaspora of Chinese from Hongkong, Taiwan and mainland China has occurred.

It is obvious to me that the nature of our literature will accordingly and inevitably change. The marvellous stories of Katherine Mansfield, writing in the earlier years of the 20th century, naturally reflect that northern European (British?) bias I have already mentioned. A scant half-century later, one could hardly say that Booker Prize-winning New Zealander, Keri Hulme, was doing the same in her equally wonderful 'The Bone People'. It may well be true to say that our greatest living writer, Janet Frame, in some ways reflects and represents the two! And so it is with our other significant writers of fiction; Maurice Gee, Fiona Kidman, C K Stead, and so on. Maori writers such as Patricia Grace, Hone Tauwhare and Witi Ihimaera inevitably reflect both the Maori and the Pakeha (Pakeha - other than Maori) worlds and how the one modifies the other. Our poets and playwrights and our writers of non-fiction often have similarly all-encompassing points of view. That the diverse nature of our New Zealand society strikes a chord in the broader 'world' sense is also evident. Many of our writers are translated into a wide variety of other languages - obviously too few into Mandarin? It is with great pleasure that I signify the recent translation by Annie Shih of NZ Christchurch Chinese writers' Association, Dr Stevan Eldred-Grigg's, 'Oracles and Miracles' - published in Shanghai and believed to be the first ever Chinese edition of a contemporary New Zealand novel. New Zealand is a tiny dot on the cultural map of the world and yet our artistic output is quite remarkably developed and, increasingly unique. Here, I speak not only of our body of literature but of our work in film, visual and graphic arts as well as in the field of performing arts. The artistic prowess of New Zealanders is every bit the equal of our (often successful!) sporting endeavours.

That our literary work 'travels' quite well is most certainly true of our writers for the young. This is, of course, my corner of the writing field. The work of our renowned children's writer, Margaret Mahy, is widely translated, as is that of Joy Cowley, Lynley Dodd and many others. My own fiction for young adults and older children is read world-wide and is translated into half a dozen other languages - including American English!! I speak of such things, not in any boastful way but, rather, to show that we are able as a very small society of just four million people, to speak with a relevance that is universal.

I said earlier in this talk that it was our responsibility to further develop the relationship between my society, the New Zealand Society of Authors, and the New Zealand/Oceania Chinese Writers' Association. That we simply extend fraternal greetings from time to time between our two associations is not enough in itself. This is as obvious to you here today as it is to me - and fully demonstrated by your invitation for me to be here with you for this conference. I am fully aware that Annie Shih has worked hard to foster an awareness of New Zealand writing here in Taiwan. Annie and Stevan Eldred- Grigg have developed a strong working relationship, resulting in the production of a series, 'New Zealand Literary History', published monthly in 'Mingdao Magazine' in Taiwan. Additionally she has profiled the work of many of our writers for the young - myself included - working in conjunction with Joan-Rosier Jones, the previous president of the NZSA. The artcles, published in the 'Mandarin Daily' provide a splendid showcase for NZ writers and writing. One of my highly treasured literary possessions is a copy of Annie's article on my novel, 'Agnes the Sheep' - in Manadarin, and of which I am unable to read much more than my name and that of the book!

Also worthy of note is the participation of the Chinese Writers' Association in one of our major literary festivals, 'Books and Beyond' in Christchurch, our third-largest city. Such practical collaboration is the stuff upon which a real literary partnership between our associations is formed. Robert Weng and others work equally hard to foster the relationship that exists between our two societies. We are, all of us, grateful for such attention. However, it is equally true to say that we, New Zealand writers and the writing and book communities in general, are insufficiently aware of the writing of Chinese writers living in NZ. This is not good enough. Sadly, the onus is more on your side than on ours, at least at first, to work to correct this situation. The reasons here are, quite simply, not those of culture in general or of not wanting to know, but of language. Many of you here today are quite well able to understand what I am saying without benefit of translation; my ignorance, and that of almost all English-speaking peoples, of other languages means that I am totally unable to converse with any of you other than in English! Oh what a sad admission indeed! Yes, certainly, we are going to need help in order to find out what you are writing. In other words, to find out more about each other. I wonder how this may be best done? I see it as my duty and pleasure over these few days to find out! Quite simply, there must be ways. Surely the natural curiosity of anyone, anywhere, who calls themself a writer is a very good foundation upon which to further build.

On a far simpler level it is important that our groups meet together socially more often. At least I am willing and certainly more able to do something about this. The ability to meet and talk about what we are doing is something we can give some thought to - and also easy enough to action! Let's do it! The New Zealand Society of Authors is structured into a half dozen branches stretching the length and breadth of our nation. Each branch meets periodically and for a variety of purposes - and often the social purpose is a main one. As writers, we all work in isolation and it is important that we, at least occasionally, get out of our solitary lives! It is my intention to find out where your members live in our country and to do what I can to further involve your writers in our association. The NZSA is, of course, not a purely social association. We work hard with government agencies, we lobby government and our arts' funding organization, (Creative NZ), in order to improve conditions for writers. In other words, we are heavily involved in the actual 'business' of writing. We also work through the main international writers' body, P.E.N. - of which we are an affiliate - on issues such as those of freedom of expression and matters of conscience. In other words, the main thrust of our work within the NZSA is along lines that affect writers everywhere. There is no reason why you should not feel welcome to join us in that work - and, of course, join with us socially. For all this, indeed everything I have said, there are more things that bind us together than keep us separate. After all, it matters less where we come from, what languages we speak and what cultural identity we either adopt or is ours by birth: It is the act of writing and the art of writing that draws us together in brotherhood and sisterhood . . . in that act and art we share the same hopes and fears; in other words, the same experience. We all work to reflect as honestly and as honourably as we can, that world in which we live.

Aotearoa New Zealand is a nation that is a reflection of many cultures and of increasing diversity. Your writers who live in New Zealand and who are New Zealanders or intending to become New Zealanders, are adding to that diversity and to the richness of our society. May your writing prosper and you, as writers, prosper accordingly. On a lighter note, I feel forced to add that although the wish is very sincere, there are not many places on this planet of ours where writers do prosper-financially!! I am positive that many of you here today also have other jobs, academic, teaching, anything you can think of that is able to provide a somewhat better level of income than writing alone. This is equally true in my own country. Few of our writers are able to make a living from writing alone!

I think I have said enough. I am more than willing to answer any questions, either now or, less formally, later in the afternoon. I have brought with me a few recent New Zealand books that you are welcome to look through - including two or three of my own. Please feel welcome to browse through them. Thank you very much for your warm welcome and a particular thank you to those who have taken the trouble to translate these words. I must refer again to your kindness and generosity in inviting me to this conference of the World Chinese Writers' Association. My visit here will live in my memory for a very long time. My very best wishes go out to

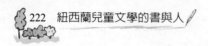

you all in your own writing endeavours. Tena koutou, tena koutou, kia ora koutou katoa. (End of Maori greeting)

William Taylor
Raurimu, New Zealand
2003

Appendix II

Agreement Establishment of Fellowship between New Zealand Society of Authors(NZSA) and Oceanian Chinese Writers' Association(OCWA)

September 2001

[RATIONALE]

Literature in a multicultural world should know no boundaries. English has become the most widely disseminated language in the world, spoken and read as a second language by more people than any other tongue. Chinese at the same time has become the language spoken by the largest population in the world. Many of the qualities and meanings intrinsic to Chinese are still hidden behind the language, however, while New Zealand literature thanks to its geographical location and short history has not been made widely available to Chinese society. Since literature and arts express human emotions in a uniquely subtle and complex way, we hope to help Chinese and New Zealand literature win popularity in both the western and eastern world beyond barriers of culture and language.

A close relationship between our two organisations has been pioneered at a regional level by the Christchurch Chinese Writers Association and the Canterbury Branch of the New Zealand Society of Authors. The relationship has proved happy. One result has been the active participation by Chinese writers and readers in the two most recent Books d Beyond Festivals in Christchurch. Another result has been a contract signed with a leading Chinese publishing house for the publication next year of a Chinese translation of a New Zealand novel.

We all, as writers, share common goals. As literature-loving and peace-loving people we should do all we can to promote the written word, books and reading and, of equal importance, promote tolerance between cultures.

[OBJECTIVES]

1. Honorary membership of the New Zealand Chinese Writers' Association will be conferred upon the President, Vice Presidents and Members of the National Council of the New Zealand Society of Authors (PEN New Zealand Inc). Honorary membership of the New Zealand Society of Authors will be conferred upon the President and Officeholders of the New Zealand Chinese Writers' Association.

2. Both organisations will try to promote the work of the other and will offer mutual assistance wherever possible.

3. Both organisations will work to promote cross-cultural understanding and appreciation.

4. Both organisations will keep each other informed on matters concerning cultural or literary activity and will encourage joint involvement where it is thought to be of mutual benefit, aiming to

become more aware of the culture of the other, acknowledging our differences and at the same time building on our common ground.

The above agreement is subject to modification and revision whenever NZSA or OCWA perceives the need to do so.

We hereby agree on the terms of the above agreement and fully support the sisterhood establishment programme.

Representative: William Taylor

New Zealand Society of Authors

(NZSA also known as NZ International Pen)

Representative: Weng Kuang

Oceanian Chinese Writers' Association (OCWA)

Writer of the Agreement: Dr Stevan Eldred-Grigg

Translated into Chinese by Annie Shih

Appendix III

New Zealand Post Book Awards
for Children and Young Adults
(2005 – 2009 Awards List)

http://christchurchcitylibraries.com/Kids/LiteraryPrizes/NZPost

- NZ Post Book of the Year

2009	The 10 PM Questions— Kate De Goldi
2008	Snake and Lizard—Joy Cowley (illustrated by Gavin Bishop)
2007	Illustrated History of the South Pacific—Marcia Stenson (non-fiction winner)
2006	Hunter —Joy Cowley (junior fiction winner)
2005	Clubs: A Lolly Leopold Story —Kate De Goldi, ifflustrated by Jacqui Colley

- NZ Post Children's Choice

2009	The Were-Nana—Melinda Szymanik & Sarah Nelisiwe Anderson
2008	The King's Bubbles—Ruth Paul (the 2nd in 2008 NZ Post Picture Book)
2007	Kiss! Kiss! Yuck! Yuck! —Kyle Mewburn, Ali Teo & John O'Reilly
2006	Nobody's Dog —Jennifer Beck & Lindy Fisher
2005	The Other Ark —Lynley Dodd

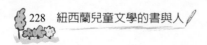

● Junior Fiction

2009	Old Drumble － Jack Lasenby
2008	Snake and Lizard－Joy Cowley
2007	Thor's Tale: Endurance and Adventure in the Southern Ocean －Janice Marriott
2006	Hunter－Joy Cowley
2005	Aunt Effie and Island that Sank －Jack Lasenby

● Young Adult Fiction

2009	The 10 PM Questions－Kate De Goldi
2008	Salt－ Maurice Gee
2007	Genesis －Bernard Beckett
2006	With Lots of Love from Georgia－Brigid Lowry
2005	Malcolm and Juliet －Bernard Beckett

● Non-Fiction

2009	Back & Beyond: New Zealand Painting for the Young and Curious－Gregory O'Brien
2008	Which New Zealand Spider －Andrew Crowe
2007	Illustrated History of the South Pacific－Marcia Stenson
2006	Scarecrow Army－Leon Davidson
2005	Welcome to the South Seas－Gregory O'Brien

- Picture Book

* 2009 Honour Award: Piggity-Wiggity Jiggity Jig—Diana Neild & Philip Webb

2009	Roadworks—Sally Sutton & Brian Lovelock
2008	Tahi— One Lucky Kiwi— Melanie Drewery, Ali Teo & John O'Reilly
2007	Kiss! Kiss! Yuck! Yuck! —Kyle Mewburn, Ali Teo & John O'Reilly
2006	A Booming in the Night —Ben Brown & Helen Taylor
2005	Clubs: A Lolly Leopold Story —Kate De Goldi, illustrated by Jacqui Colley

- Best First Book

2009	Violence 101—Denis Wright
2008	Out of the Egg—Tina Matthews (also the 3rd winner of 2008 NZ Post Picture Book)
2007	The Three Fishing Brothers Bruff —Ben Galbraith
2006	The Unknown Zone — Phil Smith
2005	Cross Tides—Lorraine Orman

國家圖書館出版品預行編目

紐西蘭兒童文學的書與人 / Joan Rosier-Jones 著; 石莉安譯.
--一版. --臺北市 : 秀威資訊科技, 2009.6
面 ; 公分. --（語言文學 ; PG0231）
BOD 版
中英對照
ISBN 978-986-221-174-8（平裝）

1.兒童文學 2.文學評論 3.紐西蘭

887.2   98002283

語言文學類　PG0231

紐西蘭兒童文學的書與人

英文作者 / Joan Rosier-Jones
中文譯者 / 石莉安
發 行 人 / 宋政坤
執行編輯 / 林世玲
圖文排版 / 陳湘陵
封面設計 / 陳佩蓉
數位轉譯 / 徐真玉　沈裕閔
圖書銷售 / 林怡君
法律顧問 / 毛國樑　律師
出版發行 / 秀威資訊科技股份有限公司
　　　　　台北市內湖區瑞光路 583 巷 25 號 1 樓
　　　　　電話：02-2657-9211　　　傳真：02-2657-9106
　　　　　E-mail：service@showwe.com.tw

2009 年 6 月 BOD 一版
定價：280 元

讀者回函卡

感謝您購買本書，為提升服務品質，請填妥以下資料，將讀者回函卡直接寄回或傳真本公司，收到您的寶貴意見後，我們會收藏記錄及檢討，謝謝！
如您需要了解本公司最新出版書目、購書優惠或企劃活動，歡迎您上網查詢或下載相關資料：http:// www.showwe.com.tw

您購買的書名：＿＿＿＿＿＿＿＿＿＿＿＿＿＿＿＿＿＿＿＿＿＿＿

出生日期：＿＿＿＿＿年＿＿＿＿＿月＿＿＿＿＿日

學歷：□高中 (含) 以下　　□大專　　□研究所 (含) 以上

職業：□製造業　□金融業　□資訊業　□軍警　□傳播業　□自由業
　　　□服務業　□公務員　□教職　　□學生　□家管　　□其它＿＿＿＿

購書地點：□網路書店　□實體書店　□書展　□郵購　□贈閱　□其他

您從何得知本書的消息？

　　□網路書店　　□實體書店　　□網路搜尋　□電子報　□書訊　□雜誌

　　□傳播媒體　　□親友推薦　　□網站推薦　□部落格　□其他＿＿＿＿＿

您對本書的評價：(請填代號　1.非常滿意　2.滿意　3.尚可　4.再改進)

　　封面設計＿＿＿　版面編排＿＿＿　內容＿＿＿　文／譯筆＿＿＿　價格＿＿＿

讀完書後您覺得：

　　□很有收穫　□有收穫　□收穫不多　□沒收穫

對我們的建議：＿＿＿＿＿＿＿＿＿＿＿＿＿＿＿＿＿＿＿＿＿＿＿

＿＿＿＿＿＿＿＿＿＿＿＿＿＿＿＿＿＿＿＿＿＿＿＿＿＿＿＿＿＿＿

＿＿＿＿＿＿＿＿＿＿＿＿＿＿＿＿＿＿＿＿＿＿＿＿＿＿＿＿＿＿＿

＿＿＿＿＿＿＿＿＿＿＿＿＿＿＿＿＿＿＿＿＿＿＿＿＿＿＿＿＿＿＿